The two Slayers sprinted down the alley together, trying to get to Balthazar's lair.

"I think we got more vamps coming!" Faith shouted. "They keep coming one at a time, we got a chance."

Just as she said it, another vampire dropped down into the alley in front of them. Faith slammed him into the wall, then tossed him across the alley. Buffy staked him without hesitation, and he was dust.

They moved on, intent upon their goal. As they rounded the corner, a hand reached out and gripped Buffy's shoulder. She grabbed the figure and threw him, hard, against a Dumpster. He cried out in pain as he hit, then slid down to the pavement.

Faith descended upon him, stake in hand.

"Faith, no!" Buffy screamed.

But it was too late. Faith punched the stake through the man's heart with a sickening crunch.

He did not dust.

He just bled.

"I didn't . . . I didn't know," Faith stammered. She shook her head, denying what her eyes saw.

It was just not possible.

Buffy the Vampire Slayer™

Buffy the Vampire Slayer (movie tie-in)	Ghoul Trouble
The Harvest	Doomsday Deck
Halloween Rain	The Angel Chronicles, Vol. 1
Coyote Moon	The Angel Chronicles, Vol. 2
Night of the Living Rerun	The Angel Chronicles, Vol. 3
Blooded	The Xander Years, Vol. 1
Visitors	The Xander Years, Vol. 2
Unnatural Selection	The Willow Files, Vol. 1
The Power of Persuasion	The Willow Files, Vol. 2
Deep Water	How I Survived My Summer Vacation, Vol. 1
Here Be Monsters	The Faith Trials, Vol. 1

Available from ARCHWAY Paperbacks and POCKET PULSE

Buffy the Vampire Slayer adult books

Child of the Hunt	Resurrecting Ravana
Return to Chaos	Prime Evil
The Gatekeeper Trilogy	The Evil That Men Do
Book 1: Out of the Madhouse	Paleo
Book 2: Ghost Roads	Spike and Dru: Pretty Maids All in a Row
Book 3: Sons of Entropy	Revenant
Obsidian Fate	The Book of Fours
Immortal	
Sins of the Father	

The Watcher's Guide, Vol. 1: The Official Companion to the Hit Show
The Watcher's Guide, Vol. 2: The Official Companion to the Hit Show
The Postcards
The Essential Angel
The Sunnydale High Yearbook
Pop Quiz: Buffy the Vampire Slayer
The Monster Book
The Script Book, Season One, Vol. 1
The Script Book, Season One, Vol. 2

Available from POCKET BOOKS

THE FAITH TRIALS

Vol. 1

A novelization by James Laurence. Based on the hit TV series
created by Joss Whedon
Based on the teleplays "Faith, Hope & Trick" by David Greenwalt,
"Bad Girls" by Douglas Petrie, and "Consequences" by Marti Noxon

POCKET PULSE
New York   London   Toronto   Sydney   Singapore

This book is a work of fiction. Names, characters, places and incidents are products of the author's imagination or are used fictitiously. Any resemblance to actual events or locales or persons, living or dead, is entirely coincidental.

An *Original* Publication of POCKET BOOKS

 POCKET PULSE, published by
Pocket Books, a division of Simon & Schuster, Inc.
1230 Avenue of the Americas, New York, NY 10020

ISBN: 0-7434-0044-5

First Pocket Pulse printing April 2001

10 9 8 7 6 5 4 3 2 1

POCKET PULSE and colophon are registered trademarks of Simon & Schuster, Inc.

Printed in the U.S.A.

Arrival

The lights of the Sunnydale Bus Terminal gleamed a sickly yellow ahead. She sat in the last seat, back to the wall, eyes always darting about in search of any threat. It was dark outside, after all, the whole world one big shadow. Sure, there was plenty of evil about when the sun was out, but it was easier to spot then. And it was only after dark that the nasties showed their ugly faces.

So she stayed alert.

Yet somehow, when the brakes on the bus shrieked as they rolled into the lot at the terminal, she felt better, like a huge weight had been lifted from her shoulders.

The bus door hissed open and she waited until nearly everyone was off before she stood and slung her bag over her shoulder. Her eyes were wide as she stepped off the bus, ignoring the lustful gaze of the driver, who'd eyed her hungrily when she had gotten on.

She strode away from the bus to the front of the station

and looked across the lot at the chain link fence and the town beyond it. *This is it*, she thought. *The place it all happens. The place to be.*

A kind of electricity seemed to hum in the air, in the ground beneath her feet, in everything. The Hellmouth was not far away, she knew. It was like a magnet, drawing demons and other creatures of darkness from around the world. But Sunnydale was also the home of Buffy Summers, the Slayer, and that fact alone kept most of the smart monsters at home.

Light and darkness. Good and evil. Chaos and order. Sunnydale was a battlefield, every night a war for the souls of its people, for the goodness in each of them.

Which she figured meant a lot of ass-kicking.

Her kind of town.

"You look lost," a deep voice drawled behind her.

She turned to find a tall, ruggedly handsome guy in leather behind her. Beyond him the bus was already pulling away to refuel and most of the passengers had either been picked up or had driven off in their own cars.

With a flirty grin, she shifted the bag on her shoulder. "I don't know. Looks like you've found me."

Mr. Rugged blinked, maybe a little surprised at her response, but then he smiled broadly. "Guess I have. You got a place to stay in town?"

"Nuh-uh." She shook her head, eyes seductively wide. She wet her lips with her tongue. "Maybe I could be down with you?"

He actually laughed. "You know, I meet a lot of girls. But I don't meet a lot of girls like you. Walk with me to my car? I can hook you up. Maybe get you a job, too, if you need money."

"I'll bet you can," she told him.

While she followed him to the car, she slipped a hand

inside her bag. He went to the passenger door and dug into a pocket for his keys.

"What's your name?"

"Faith."

"Pretty."

"Yeah. Sucks, doesn't it? I wish it was something more, I don't know, imposing. Meaner. Like Kali or Shiva or something. Though I think Shiva was a male deity. Still, I like the sound of it. Know what Shiva was called?"

He unlocked the door, then turned to face her, expression a bit uncertain now. "Can't say I do."

Faith smiled sweetly. "Destroyer of worlds."

Her left hand lashed out and gripped his throat and she slammed his back against the car, shattering a window. His face underwent a savage metamorphosis, became more feral, his fangs protruding.

"Vampires," she said disgustedly. "I'm surprised any of you have the guts to hang around this town, what with the Slayer here. I'm guessing you're just stupid. Either that, or you're the bottom of the barrel and she hasn't had time to get around to you yet. I mean, come on, picking up runaways at the bus station? That's so . . . what's that friggin' word? Cliché? That's it. You're a cliché."

"But . . . but . . ." the vampire sputtered. "I've seen her. You're not her! Who the hell are you?"

"I told you," she snapped angrily. Then she head-butted him with a crack that echoed in the empty lot. "I'm Faith."

With a grunt, she thrust the stake through his heart and the vampire exploded in a shower of dust. Faith moved her head side to side, stretching her neck muscles, stiff from the long bus ride. She slipped the stake back into her bag and brushed vampire dust off her pants.

Then she turned and started to walk away from the station, into Sunnydale. It was a new start for her.

A whole new life.

But even as she disappeared into the shadows, she was aware that it was only a matter of time before her old life reared its ugly head.

FAITH, HOPE &
TRICK

Prologue

I'm giddy," Willow Rosenberg said, a tiny smirk crinkling the corners of her mouth. She rocked a little on her feet, standing at the edge of the curb.

Oz looked at her appreciatively. "I like you giddy. Always have."

They stood side by side on the sidewalk at the outer limits of the grounds of Sunnydale High School, paused there as if frozen, or just waiting for something. In this case, that something would be waiting for Willow to move.

"It's the freedom," Willow told her boyfriend. "As seniors we can go off campus now for lunch. It's no longer cutting, it's legal. Heck, it's expected. But also a big step forward, a Senior Moment. One that has to be savored. You can't just rush into this, y'know?"

Oz glanced over his shoulder to see Xander Harris sauntering up behind Willow with his girlfriend, Cordelia Chase. The two guys exchanged nods and as Xander swept up to them, they grabbed Willow under her arms and carried her off the sidewalk.

"Ooo!" Willow exclaimed. "No! I can't."

"You can," Xander told her patiently as they propelled her along with them into the street.

"See, you are," Oz said, pointing out the fact that her feet were moving, no matter how reluctantly.

Cordelia, aloof in dark sunglasses and a red and black summer dress, walked along as though only half willing to admit she was with them.

"But what if they changed the rule without telling?" Willow said, still resisting. "What if they're lying in wait to arrest me and throw me in detention and mar my un-blemished record?"

"Breathe," Xander instructed her. "Breathe."

Willow did as he asked, pausing in the street to take a breath. She calmed herself and linked arms with Oz. Xan-der slung an arm around Cordelia and the two couples moved on.

"Okay," Willow said. "This is good. This is—hey! We're seniors. Hey, I'm walkin' here!"

On a tiny parklike common area across the street, other seniors milled about, studying and eating lunch. The foursome spotted Buffy Summers in front of a wooden bench, laying out a picnic on a red and white checkered tablecloth she'd spread on the grass. Their friend had had a great deal of trouble at the end of the previous school year and had been suspended. Buffy's mother was trying to get her back in, but in the meanwhile, she was an out-sider where school was concerned.

"Ah, Buffy and food," Xander announced happily.

Willow was troubled, however. "Maybe we shouldn't be too couply around Buffy."

"Oh, you mean 'cause of how the only guy that ever liked her turned into a vicious killer and had to be put down like a dog?" Cordelia replied bluntly.

Though she was the vampire Slayer, Buffy had been in

love with a vampire named Angel, unique because, unlike other vampires, he had a human soul. When that soul was taken from him, he became evil like others of his kind and attempted to open a portal into Hell. To save the world, Buffy had been forced to kill him and send him through that portal. It had devastated her. Only now did she seem to be dealing with it.

Xander glanced at Cordelia, then at the others. "Can she cram complex issues into a nutshell, or what?" he asked proudly.

No response was forthcoming, however. The foursome was approaching the spot where Buffy had laid out the picnic.

"All right, prepare to uncouple," Oz instructed, almost under his breath. "Uncouple."

At that, Willow let go of Oz's hand and Xander broke away from Cordelia. The four of them spread out as they approached Buffy.

With a soft smile on her face, Buffy saw her friends coming across the lawn. Oz wore a checked shirt over an orange tee and dark pants, the clothes hanging in a way that should have looked messy but didn't on him. Willow had on a fuzzy blue shirt and red jeans, her simple neatness a perfect complement to her boyfriend. Though he had sneakers on his feet, Xander wore a black and white bowling shirt that looked pretty snazzy on him. His clothing choices had improved dramatically once he had started to date Cordelia. As for Queen C. herself, she was a fashion plate, as usual.

It was great to see them. Buffy felt so detached when they were in school and she wasn't—not that she missed the learning, even though it was a necessary evil—and this had been a nice way to deal with that. She'd gotten a bit dressed up, herself. A beige summer dress with a subtle floral pattern and a light shirt thrown over her shoulders.

"Buffy!" Xander said amiably. "Banned from campus but not from our hearts. How are ya and what's for lunch?"

She smiled as they all sat on the ground around her. "Oh, I just threw a few things together."

"When did you become Martha Stewart?" Cordelia said, impressed despite herself.

"First of all, Martha Stewart knows jack about hand-cut prosciutto," Buffy replied.

Xander nodded thoughtfully. "I don't believe she slays, either."

"I hear she can, but she doesn't like to," Oz put in.

Paying no attention to their remarks, Buffy went on. "Second of all, way too much time on my hands since I got kicked out of school." A bit sad, she glanced away as she sipped from a bottle of water.

"Oh, I know they'll let you back in," Willow told her.

"Don't you and your mom have a meeting with Principal Snyder?" Xander asked.

"We're seeing Snyde Man tomorrow," Buffy confirmed.

She looked at Willow, but her best friend had obviously spotted something of interest across the small park.

"Ooh, Scott Hope at eleven o' clock," Willow pointed out.

Buffy turned to see Scott talking to some friends. With dark hair and a sweet smile, he was more than cute.

"He likes you," Willow told her. "He wanted to ask you out last year, but you weren't ready then. But I think you're ready now—or at least in the state of pre-readiness to make conversation or do that thing with your mouth that boys like—"

Buffy stared at her in shock.

"Oh, I didn't mean that bad thing with your mouth, I meant that little half-smile thing that you . . ." she fumbled, then gazed pleadingly up at Oz. "You're s'posed to stop me when I do that."

Oz was cool as ever. "I like when you do that," he said.

Scott had walked away from his friends and was now moving in their general direction. As he passed he looked over at Buffy with a shy smile.

"Hi, Buffy," he said.

She felt a bit shy herself. "Hi."

"I think that went very well," Willow said happily. "Don't you think that went very well?"

"He didn't try to slit our throats or anything," Cordelia said reasonably. "It's progress."

"Hey, did you do that little half-smile thing?" Willow asked Buffy.

"Look, I'm not trying to snare Scott Hope," Buffy replied, reluctant to burst her friend's bubble. "I just want to get my life back, y'know? Do normal stuff."

"Like date," Willow prodded.

"Well . . ." Buffy was about to argue the point when Xander cut in.

"Oh, you wanna date," he said, mouth filled with picnic munchies. "I saw that half-smile, you little slut."

Buffy gave him a quick shot to the arm. The grin of amusement on Xander's face disappeared after a moment, a delayed reaction.

"Ow," he protested.

"All right, yes. Date and shop and hang out and go to school and save the world from unspeakable demons. Y'know, I wanna do girlie stuff."

Night had fallen on Sunnydale, California by the time the long limousine with its blacked out windows rolled into the parking lot of Happy Burger. The fast-food restaurant's neon signs and plastic mascot were garishly bright. The near-silent limo cruised up to the hideous mascot—a hamburger-man sinking sharp teeth into a blood-red burger—and a voice came from the menu board behind it.

"Welcome to Happy Burger, can I take your order, please?"

In the dark recesses of the plush backseat of the limousine, Mr. Trick leaned slightly forward. "Diet soda. Medium."

"That'll be eighty-nine cents at the window, sir," the electronic voice came back.

Trick hit the button to roll up the tinted window and sat back into the soft seat again, aware as always of the ominous presence beside him. His eyes ticked right but he was reluctant to look at Kakistos for too long. His employer was far from easy on the eyes, never mind the sense of menace that exuded from him. Kakistos was a vampire, but far, far older and more powerful than Trick.

"Sunnydale," Mr. Trick said, glancing out the window again as the limo rolled up toward the takeout window. He looked at Kakistos and smiled. "Town's got quaint, and the people? He called me sir, don't you just miss that? Admittedly, it's not a haven for the brothers— strictly the Caucasian persuasion here in the 'Dale—but you just gotta stand up and salute that death rate. I ran a statistical analysis and Hello Darkness. Makes D.C. look like Mayberry. And ain't nobody sayin' boo about it. We could fit right in here. Have us some fun."

Unamused, Kakistos leaned slightly forward, the leather seat crinkling beneath his shifting weight. The lights from Happy Burger shone on the pink scar that ran down the right side of his face. One of his heavy cloven hands rested on Trick's knee.

"We're here for one thing," the vampire rumbled.

Trick swallowed nervously. "Kill the Slayer, yeah. Still, big picture . . ."

In the takeout window, the Happy Burger employee was ready with Trick's soda. The vampire was glad for the interruption. He rolled the window down again and reached out to take his drink.

"Have a nice night, sir," the teenager said.

"Right back atcha," Trick replied, still pleased by the manners of the locals.

"The Slayer," Kakistos snarled, not yet ready to move on to another subject. "I'm going to rip her spine from her body, and I'm going to eat her heart and suck the marrow from her bones."

Trick sighed. "Now I'm hungry."

His features shifted in an instant to the horrid countenance of the vampire. With a single motion he reached out of the limo and grabbed hold of the takeout guy's uniform shirt, then dragged him out screaming. Glass shattered as Trick hauled him into the backseat of the limo.

As the limousine sped from the parking lot of the Happy Burger, he feasted on the polite young man's blood.

Now that's service, Trick thought, his features splitting into a crimson grin.

CHAPTER 1

The Bronze.

An absolutely perfect night at Buffy's all-time favorite hangout with her buds. Cordelia, Xander, Oz, and Willow sat at a table and watched her as she danced.

Danced.

With Angel.

The music pounded out a subtle rhythm. Her friends did not smile at her. She felt a tiny shudder go through her as a horrible suspicion crossed her mind. Buffy pushed it away. She needed the strength of his hands on her to be real, needed him with her.

Moving slowly with Angel, she glanced up at him sadly. Their foreheads touched as they nuzzled together just a bit.

"I miss you," she whispered.

Her hands moved down along his arms and her fingers twined with his. The claddagh ring on her left hand—the ring he had given her as a promise that he would always be with her—slipped from her finger and hit the floor with a tinkling metallic sound. Slowly, Buffy and Angel both glanced down at it.

Angel reached down to pick it up. When his fingers touched it, he flinched. His gaze burned her like fire and guilt swept over her. He stared at her and she knew he remembered that she had run him through with a sword, sent him plunging through a portal into Hell eternal, in order to save the world.

Heart breaking, Buffy shook her head slowly. "I had to," she said weakly.

Angel crushed the ring in his right hand, the one upon which he wore its twin, and blood dripped from between his fingers.

"I loved you," he said, though his voice quavered with anger.

His white shirt blossomed with a spreading bloodstain, right at the spot where the sword had punched through his chest.

"Oh God, Angel," Buffy cried, reaching out for him.

"Go to Hell!" he snapped, furious.

Buffy glanced at the bloodstain again. Then she heard him chuckling softly, cruelly, and her gaze went back to his face.

A horrible face. Dead. Decaying. The rotting face of a corpse.

Buffy's eyes flickered open. She sat up in bed, heart aching with the echoes of her dream, deeply troubled. It had all felt so real. But then again, the worst dreams always did.

She reached over and opened the nightstand drawer. Inside was the claddagh ring Angel had given her, hung from a chain. She pulled it out and was still staring at it when her mother rapped on the open door to her bedroom.

"Morning, Sunshine," Joyce Summers said pleasantly. "Ready to face the Beast?"

A short time later, Buffy and her mother sat in the office of the Beast—Principal Snyder—as the cantankerous, bitter man glared at them from his high-backed desk chair. Buffy reached out to pick up a silver, daggerlike letter opener from his desk and fiddled with it, a bit nervous.

"Here are the terms of your reentry, Miss. Take 'em or leave 'em," Snyder said, anger simmering beneath his words. "One, that you pass a makeup test for every class you skipped out on last year. Two, that you provide, in writing, one glowing letter of recommendation from any member of our faculty who is not an English librarian."

Snyder eyed the letter opener in Buffy's hands and rose from his chair. He continued to speak as he moved around his desk toward her.

"Three, that you complete an interview with our school psychologist, who must conclude that your violent tendencies are under control." Snyder snatched the letter opener from Buffy's hands and glared at her.

"I'm not sure I like your attitude, Mr. Snyder," Joyce said tersely. "I spoke to the school board and according to them—"

"I'm required to educate every juvenile who's not in jail where she belongs," the principal interrupted. He crossed the room and stared petulantly out the window. "Welcome back."

Buffy stood up and eyed him with amusement. "So let me get this straight. I'm really back because the school board overruled you. Wow, that's like having your whole ability to do this job called into question, when you think about it."

Her mother stood up beside her. "I think what my daughter's trying to say is, nyah nyah nyah nyah."

Satisfied, the two Summers women stood up and strode from Snyder's office.

Just after they'd shut the door behind them, the intercom on Snyder's desk buzzed.

"It's the Mayor on line one," his secretary informed him.

Snyder glanced down at the intercom anxiously as a feeling of dread swept over him.

With the weight of her suspension gone, Buffy felt happier than she had in weeks. Even the fact that Giles had sent Willow to find her—which probably meant she had done something wrong—could not erase that good feeling. Side by side, she and Willow breezed along the hallways of Sunnydale High as if she had never left. As they pushed through the doors into the library, Willow seemed almost happier than Buffy.

"It's so great that you're a schoolgirl again," Willow said.

Buffy glanced around the library, but they seemed to be alone. "Did Giles say what he wanted?" she asked. "Do you think he's mad?"

"No, I don't think so. I think he just needed to see you. Have you ever noticed though, when he *is* mad but he's too English to say anything, he makes that weird 'cluck cluck' sound with his tongue?"

Willow grinned but did not notice Giles rise from behind the library checkout counter with a mortar and pestle and a bowl of some odd concoction. He had apparently been retrieving something from under the counter, but had clearly heard every word.

"Hi, Giles!" Buffy chirped awkwardly.

Eyes wide with surprise, Willow turned around. "Oh, hi. Been there long?"

Giles paid no attention to the question. "Buffy, good

timing," he said absently. "I could use your help. I trust you remember the demon Acathla."

"Giles, contain yourself," Buffy replied, voice dripping with sarcasm. "Yes, I'm back in school but you know how it embarrasses me when you gush, so let's just skip all that and get straight to work."

Caught off guard, Giles fumbled for a response. "Oh, ahhh, of course it's wonderful to have you back. That goes without saying. But you . . . enjoy making me say it, don't you?"

She did enjoy seeing him squirm. Buffy grinned.

"Okay, Acathla, huh? What are ya doin'?" she asked, gesturing toward the mortar and pestle on the counter. "Making him some demon pizza?"

"We need to make sure he remains dormant, and that the dimensional vortex is sealed tight. So I'm working on a binding spell."

At the mention of a spell, Willow perked up. "Ooo, a spell, can I help?"

Buffy's best friend was a spellcaster-in-training, but Giles was always cautious about letting Willow get ahead of herself. Magick could be very dangerous when wielded by a novice. Buffy had heard Giles tell her that a hundred times.

"Possibly with the research. It's a very sensitive—"

"Who's more sensitive than me?" Willow asked in protest.

"—and difficult spell," Giles finished. "It involves a protective circle around . . . well, I don't want to bore you, but there's litany that one has to recite in Aramaic and it's very specific. So I need to get a few details about your experiences in defeating Acathla and Angel."

Buffy felt a twinge of pain and guilt as she recalled her last moments with Angel and her dream from that morning. With a heavy heart, she looked up at Giles.

"Fire away."

"I've put the time at about six-seventeen? About half an hour after Xander rescued me."

"Less. More like ten minutes."

"Was the vortex already open?"

"Barely." Buffy felt cold.

The Watcher's expression was troubled. "I see. And Angel?"

"Big fight. Angel got the pointy end of the sword. Acathla sucked him into Hell instead of the world. That's about it."

"Yes, well that, um, should be very helpful," Giles said softly.

With a flash of alarm, Buffy glanced at her watch. "Oh, no. I have to go take an English makeup exam." She paused at the door and looked back at them. "They give you credit for just speaking it, right?"

At the pitying looks she received from Giles and Willow, Buffy moaned and rushed off to her exam.

After Buffy left, Willow picked up a small bundle of herbs Giles had put on the counter. She smiled as she inhaled deeply.

"Mmm. Sage. I love that smell. And Marnox root? You know a smidgen of this mixed with a virgin's saliva—"

Giles cast her a baleful glance.

"—does something I know nothing about," Willow finished sheepishly.

"These forces are not something that one plays around with, Willow," Giles warned. "What have you been conjuring?"

"Nothing!" she protested innocently, then faltered. "Much. Well, you know, I tried the spell to cure Angel and I guess that was a bust. But since then, you know, small stuff. Floating feather, fire out of ice, which next time I won't do on the bedspread." She glanced up at him anxiously. "Are you mad at me?"

"No, of course not," Giles replied. "If I were, I would be making a strange clucking sound with my tongue."

Despite the awkwardness of her conversation earlier in the day with Giles, by the time Buffy hit the Bronze with Willow and Oz that night she was nearly giddy. Even the echo of her dream the night before could not taint her feeling that everything was going right for a change.

The Bronze was packed. Darling Violetta cranked out a sultry melody on the stage as people danced all around. Buffy had gotten drinks for the three of them and when she went back to the table, Willow and Oz were trading soft kisses.

"Don't let me interrupt," she said with a smile.

"Are you—" Willow began, then turned to Oz. "Is she all a glow-y?"

Oz nodded. "I suspect happiness."

"I passed my English makeup exam. I'm hanging with my friends." Buffy's smile grew even wider. "Hello my life, how I've missed you."

As if on cue, Scott Hope strolled up to their table. Willow grinned at him.

"Hi, Scott, what are you doing here?" she asked.

Almost shyly, Scott shrugged. "You told me if I came after eight I could run into Buffy," he replied, before focusing on Buffy. "I'm sorry, I'm a bad liar. It's not good for the soul. Or the skin, actually. It makes me blotch."

Though she felt awkward, Buffy was charmed by him. "Hi, Scott."

"Hi," he replied, obviously relieved. "Don't you love this song?"

"Uh, yeah. Actually I do."

"Well, would you like to—"

"Dance?" Buffy finished for him, feeling a kind of panic rising in her. "I, uh . . . I don't know. I'm bad with, well . . . thank you for asking, it's just that . . ."

Scott took a breath. "Okay, you know what? I'm just going to go stand by the dance floor. If you change your mind you can mosey on over. And if not, then, you don't mosey. No harm, no foul, right?"

"Right," Buffy said sadly.

Scott walked off and Buffy looked over to see Willow staring at her.

"Come on, Buffy," Willow said. "I mean, the guy is charm. And normal, which you wanted to get back to."

"Plus, bonus points for use of the word *mosey*," Oz added.

Buffy knew they were right, but that didn't help. In some ways, it made her feel worse. "I just don't think I'm ready."

"What's stopping you?" Willow asked, concern in her voice.

Before Buffy could answer, Cordelia and Xander arrived to join them at the table. Cordelia wore a killer red dress that was certain to draw stares from many of the guys in the Bronze.

"Check out the slut-o-rama and her Disco Dave," she said as she and Xander sat down. "What was the last thing that guy danced to, K.C. and the Sunshine Band?"

Buffy gazed out at the sea of bodies thrashing about on the dance floor of the Bronze. She identified the objects of Cordelia's scorn immediately. The girl was a handful and a half, dressed in a tight, belly-baring black tank and leopard print pants that were even tighter. She danced the way she dressed, like something wild.

The guy was a different story. If Buffy didn't know better, she would have guessed his hideous brown-and-beige shirt and pants were polyester. He danced like he'd just seen *Saturday Night Fever* for the first time. Buffy frowned as she watched him. And then she knew.

Like the girl, he danced and dressed like what he was. A child of the seventies. But he still looked no more than nineteen.

Which meant only one thing.

Vampire.

"I don't think that guy thrives on sunshine," she said.

Even as she came to that realization, the vampire and his wild girl left the dance floor and headed for the exit. Buffy sprang up from the table instantly and followed them. As she crossed the club, headed for the door, she found Scott Hope at the edge of the dance floor, waiting for her, just as he'd said he would.

"Hi," he said hopefully, a broad smile on his face.

"Hi," Buffy replied. Then, realizing he thought she'd come to dance with him, she fumbled. "Oh. No, I have to—"

A hurt look in his eyes. "Oh. Sorry. My bad."

"No. It's mine. Really, it's mine. But I have to go—" She felt awful, but she strode past him and out the door of the Bronze.

Willow and the others weren't far behind.

The five of them stood out in front of the club and looked around at the shadows and dark alleys nearby, but no one was in sight.

"Where'd she go?" Buffy asked.

Cordelia grumbled. "I bet it's nothing. They're probably just making out."

From off to the right they heard a shout and a commotion, like a struggle going on.

"That's not what making out sounds like," Willow said as they all ran toward the source of the noise. "Unless I'm doing it wrong."

Stake in hand, Buffy led the group around a corner into

an alley just in time to see the wild girl drive the vampire to the ground with a powerful side kick. The girl's raven hair flew as she turned toward them. When she saw them, she smiled and sauntered over.

"It's okay, I got it," she said, as though fighting vampires were the simplest thing in the world. "You're Buffy, right?"

The vampire leaped from the ground and lunged at the girl from behind. It grabbed her, but she rammed her head back to smash into its face.

"I'm Faith."

Faith grabbed the vampire's arm, twisted, and slammed it into a chain link fence.

"I'm gonna go out on a limb here and say there's a new Slayer in town," Oz observed dryly.

With a cold brutality, Faith battered the vampire. She reached out to grab the stake in Buffy's hand.

"Can I borrow that?"

Another two hard blows and she slammed the blood-sucker back up against the fence, then staked it. The vampire exploded into dust. Faith turned and smiled at them as she handed the stake back to Buffy.

"Thanks, B. Couldn't have done it without you."

CHAPTER 2

Buffy was a bit shell-shocked. After Faith dusted the vampire, they had all come back into the Bronze and managed to score another table. Now the entire gang was gathered around listening to Faith ramble about her exploits, hanging on her every word. Not that Buffy was envious or anything. It was just that this new arrival had a very powerful personality, was ultra-sexy in that trampy, trashy way, and had a confident swagger Buffy had never felt in herself.

As she listened to Faith go on, Buffy tried to put her hesitations aside. The girl was a Slayer, after all. Liking her was sort of required. It felt like her duty to at least try to get along.

"The whole summer it was like the worst heat wave," Faith was saying. "So it's about a hundred and eighteen degrees and I'm sleeping without a stitch on. And all of a sudden I hear this screaming from outside. So I go tearin' out—stark nude—and this church bus has broke down and there's these three vamps feasting on half the Baptists in South Boston. So I waste the vamps and the preacher comes up and he's hugging me like there's no tomorrow when all of a sudden the cops pull up. They arrested us both."

Xander gaped at her in undisguised admiration. "Wow! They should film that story and show it every Christmas."

Faith picked up a roll from the table and started nibbling at it. "God, I could eat a horse! Isn't it crazy how slaying just always makes you hungry and horny."

Buffy felt her friends staring at her, waiting for her response to Faith's bold declaration. She glanced around sheepishly. "Well . . . sometimes I crave a non-fat yogurt afterward."

"I get it!" Cordelia said suddenly. This time they all looked at her, and she scowled in disgust. "Not the horny thing. Yuck. But the two Slayer thing? There was one, and then Buffy died for like two minutes so then Kendra was called. Then when she died, Faith was called."

Willow frowned. "But why were you called here?"

"I wasn't," Faith explained. "My Watcher went off to some retreat thing in England, and so I skipped out. I figured this was my big chance to meet the infamous Buff and compare notes." Faith turned her attention to Buffy. "So B, did you really use a rocket launcher one time?"

Buffy was taken aback momentarily when Faith turned the focus back to her. Then she shrugged, a bit self-conscious. "Yeah, actually, it's a funny story—"

"So what was the story about that alligator?" Xander interrupted. "You said something before."

All her friends had heard her stories before. Or had been there for the actual real-life happenings. Buffy sank deeper into her chair as the spotlight went back to Faith.

"Oh, there's this big daddy vampire out of Missouri who used to keep 'em as pets. So he's got me rasslin' one of 'em, the thing must've been twelve feet long—"

Enthralled, Xander gazed at Faith. "Now, was this also naked?"

Obviously pleased with the attention, Faith smiled flirtatiously at him. "Well, the alligator was . . ."

Beside him, Cordelia had her arms crossed as she glared daggers at him. "Xander, find a new theme."

For her part, though, Faith wasn't paying attention. Her mind was still on the story she had begun to tell. "I'll tell ya, I never had more trouble than that damn vamp," she said idly. Then her attention was back on Buffy. "So what about you? What was your toughest kill?"

Buffy blinked. Though the intention of Faith's question was obviously something else entirely, her mind again went to Angel, to the moment in which she had run him through with that gleaming sword. She shook it off, and tried to think of something else.

"Well, y'know they're all difficult, I guess. Oh, do you guys remember the Three? That's right, you never met the Three. Well, there were three—"

Once again, Buffy was interrupted, though this time it was Oz who cut in.

"Something occurring," he drawled. "Now, you both kill vamps and who could blame you, but I'm wondering about your position on werewolves."

Faith raised her eyebrows.

"Oz is a werewolf," Willow added, before she could respond.

"It's a long story," Buffy explained.

The werewolf in question gave a tiny nod. "Got bit."

"Apparently not that long," Buffy corrected herself.

Faith seemed unperturbed. "Hey, as long as you don't go scratching at me or humpin' my leg, we're five by five, y'know?"

"Fair enough," Oz replied.

The newly-arrived Slayer grinned at Buffy. "The

vamps, though, they better get their asses to Def-Con One. 'Cause you and I are gonna have fun, y'know? Watcher-less and fancy free."

Buffy frowned. "Watcher-less?"

"Didn't yours go to England, too?"

The next morning, in the library, Giles stood with his back to them, a sense of melancholy radiating from him. With a sigh, he turned to face them. "There is a Watchers' retreat every year in the Cotswolds. It's a lovely spot, very serene. There's horse riding and hiking and punting, and lectures and discussions. It's quite an honor to be invited. Or so I'm told."

He gazed off at nothing, a sadness in his eyes.

"Ah, it's boring," Faith put in. "Way too stuffy for a guy like you."

Buffy stared at her as though she were mad. "Um, maybe I should introduce you again. Faith, this is Giles."

Faith nodded appreciatively. "I seen him. If I'd'a known they came that young and cute I'd've requested a transfer."

Horrified, Buffy turned to Xander and Willow, who sat on the study table in the center of the library. "Raise your hand if *eew*."

"Well, leaving for the moment the question of my youth and beauty, I would say it's fortuitous that Faith arrived when she did," Giles said, a bit flustered by Faith's attention.

"Ah-hah!" Willow exclaimed. When they all looked at her, she seemed to deflate a bit. "Sorry, I just meant—ah-hah! There's big evil brewing. You'll never be bored here, Faith, 'cause this is Sunnydale, home of the big brewing evil."

Giles retrieved a newspaper from the counter behind him and handed it to the two Slayers. "Yes, well, I don't know how big an evil it is, but two people have disappeared from the Sunset Ridge district."

Together, Buffy and Faith glanced at the article. After a moment, Buffy looked up at her Watcher.

"Well, I'm good for patrolling," she said. "Lateish, though. I promised Mom I'd be home for dinner."

Xander looked at her expectantly. Willow even nodded in Faith's direction. At first Buffy didn't get it, and when she did she wished she had not. At length, she turned reluctantly to Faith.

"To which you're also invited, of course. Dinner with us."

"Dying to meet the fam. I'm in," Faith said pleasantly.

"Great," Buffy replied, attempting to sound happy about the prospect. "Great. Then we can patrol. Also together."

"Hey, don't you have that health science makeup?" Willow asked suddenly.

"Oh, yeah, actually. I could use a little coaching—" Buffy began.

Willow did not hear her, though. Her focus was on Faith.

"Y'know, you can hang with us while she's testing. You wanta?" Willow asked.

"Say yes and bring your stories," Xander prodded.

"You guys go," Buffy reassured them. Not as if they needed it, however. She wondered if the sarcasm she felt was apparent in her tone of voice. "It's fine. I'll just sit."

"Okay," Faith agreed. She gave Buffy a tiny wave. "Hey, later." Then she pointed at Giles. "We'll talk weapons."

Forlorn and feeling more than a little abandoned, Buffy sat at the study table and watched them all go. A moment later Giles came to lean against the table.

"This new girl seems to have a lot of zest," the Watcher observed. Then he frowned. "Oh, I've been having a little problem with the binding spell for Acathla. I'm lacking the requisite details to perform it correctly. Now, the physical location: Acathla was facing south?"

Though that night was her least favorite subject, Buffy drew a tiny diagram on the table with her finger. "Uh-huh. Acathla. Angel. Me. Sword."

"See, that's what I thought, but—"

Buffy stood up abruptly. "Giles, look, I've got makeup tests to pass, missing people in Sunset Ridge, and a zesty new Slayer to feed. Next time I kill Angel I'll video it."

She slipped on her backpack and left the library as if running away from something.

Faith felt more than a little out of place in the burgundy leather pants she wore, but out of place in a good way. Sunnydale High students didn't share her fashion sense. Not that the kids in South Boston did either. Still, Willow and Xander seemed nice enough as they gave her the grand tour.

"And here we have the cafeteria, where we were mauled by snakes," Willow informed her, in an offhanded way, as if that sort of thing happened to her every day.

Faith was getting the idea that maybe around her it did.

"This is the spot where Angel tried to kill Willow," Xander added.

"Oh, and over there in the lounge is where Spike and his gang nearly massacred us all on parent-teacher night," Willow continued, almost as though the two were trying to one-up each other. "Oh, and up those stairs, I was sucked into a muddy grave."

"And they say young people don't learn anything in high school nowadays," Xander mused. "But I've learned to be afraid."

Faith paused in the hall and turned to them. "You guys are a hoot and a half. I mean, if I'd had friends like you in high school . . . I probably still would've dropped out, but I mighta been sad about it."

Willow and Xander smiled.

Feeling as though she had made a connection with the two, Faith forged ahead.

"Hey, so what's up with B? I mean, she seems wound kinda tight, needs to find the fun a little, like you two."

Just as Willow began to respond, Faith saw a fountain across the hall. "Oh, water," she said, almost to herself as she went for a drink.

"And then the alligator story," Xander reminded her. Then, when he thought she was out of earshot, he added: "She's got something, doesn't she?"

Faith smiled to herself, for even as he said it, his girl-friend Cordelia came up behind him.

"What is it with you and Slayers?" she demanded. "Maybe I should dress up as one and put a stake to your throat."

"Please, God, don't let that be sarcasm," Xander said excitely.

Amused, Faith turned away from the fountain and almost ran into a cute, dark-haired guy.

"Oh, excuse me," he said.

Faith smiled. "Sorry. I know you from somewhere."

He thought for a moment, then pointed at her. "The Bronze? You're friends with Buffy, right?"

"Yeah. I'm Faith."

"I'm Scott. Nice to meet you."

"Nice to meet you, too."

Buffy came down the stairs at a trot when she spotted Willow, Xander and Cordelia standing in the hall. "Well, I'm two for two with the makeup tests," she said. "Proud, yes, but also humble in this time of . . . we're looking at what?"

Across the hall, she spotted Faith flirting and laughing with Scott Hope. A sick feeling burned its way through her. That, of course, was what her friends had been looking at. So obviously she wasn't the only one who felt uncomfortable about it. Not that she had a right to, but *still.*

"Does anyone believe that is her actual hair color?" Cordelia asked cattily.

Willow, on the other hand, seemed pleased. "I haven't seen him laugh like that. Hey, maybe Faith and Scott could hit it off." When she glanced at Buffy, however, Willow's smile disappeared. "That is, if you're done with him." She thought about what she said and her expression became even more crestfallen. "Not that you used him . . ."

"Well, I hadn't definitely one hundred percent said no for all time," Buffy confessed. "It's just, you don't enter into these things lightly, y'know. There's repercussions to consider, and . . ."

As she spoke, she looked at her friends. Xander and Willow were both gazing at her with tired expressions.

"Why am I seeing a look?" Buffy demanded.

Willow sighed. "You really do need to find the fun, B . . . uffy!"

Appalled by her friend's use of Faith's annoying nickname for her, Buffy turned and strode over to where the other Slayer was still flirting with Scott.

"Hey," she said.

"Hey, Buffy," Scott said amiably. "Faith has been telling me tall tales."

"She's funny," Buffy deadpanned. "And she's leaving. We have to go."

"Oh. Bye," Scott said.

As Buffy dragged her away, Faith leaned over to her. "He's a cutie," she said. "Is he seeing anybody?"

In an abandoned firehouse in an unsavory section of Sunnydale, vampires lit candles, swung iron censers filled with incense, and chanted the name of their dark lord. Mr. Trick was not at all fond of his employer's choice of lairs. He would have been much happier at a luxury hotel. But elder vampires—the old-timers, as he thought of them—had a taste for doing things the old-fashioned way.

Though there were many candles, the overhead lights still worked in the firehouse. They shone down upon the master vampire's scarred face. Kakistos glanced up as Trick approached.

"Mr. Trick," Kakistos rasped as the vampire strode past the parked limousine toward him. "Talk to me."

"Check this out," Trick replied excitedly. "This town. This very street. Wired for fiber optics. We jack in a T-3, twenty five hundred megs per, we have the whole world at our fingertips. All I'm saying is, we stay local, where the humans are jumping and the cotton is high, but we live global. You got the hankering for the blood of a fif-teen-year-old Filipina? I'm on the Net and she's here the next day, express air."

Kakistos was unimpressed. An animal rumbling sound rolled from his throat as he spoke. "I want the blood of the Slayer."

Trick sighed. "On that note, there's good news and bad. Rumor has it that this town already has a Slayer, which makes two. I'm not sure how that happens."

With a growl, Kakistos surged from his chair and stood glaring with his one good eye and the white, scar-crossed one, down at Mr. Trick. "I don't care if there are a hundred Slayers!" he snapped. "I'll kill them all!" With the thumb of one of his hideous, cloven hands, he pointed toward the scar. "She's going to pay for what she did to me."

Grimly, Trick nodded. "Yeah, she is. I'm running a computer check on every hotel, rooming house and youth hostel in town."

There was a knock at the door. In response, Trick walked over to a table and slipped on a huge rubber glove left over from the days when the place was still an operational firehouse.

"Meanwhile," he told Kakistos, "as soon as the sun goes down, we're out in force."

Another knock, and Trick sauntered toward the door. He glanced at the other vampires around him. "Food's here, boys."

He opened the door, his hand protected from the harsh sunlight by the glove. Outside, a delivery man held a pizza box.

"Hey," the man said. "You guys order a—"

Trick reached out and hauled him inside. He threw the man down and then fell upon him, fangs bared. The pizza lay to one side, forgotten. The others would have a taste after Trick was through.

In the dining room of the Summers home, Joyce served dinner to her daughter and the new friend she'd brought home. She enjoyed cooking for guests, and this Faith seemed like a very sweet girl. It had come as a bit of a shock to her that there was another Slayer, but then, there was very little about what Buffy did that Joyce didn't find shocking.

"So you're a Slayer too," she said as she served the squash. "Isn't that interesting? Do you like it?"

"I love it," Faith replied without hesitation.

"Um, Mom?" Buffy ventured, indicating the unpassed squash.

"Just a second, honey," Joyce said, fascinated by what Faith was saying. She put some broccoli on the girl's plate as well. "You know, Buffy never talks that way. Why do you love it?"

Faith shrugged. "Well, when I'm fighting it's like the whole world goes away and I only know one thing; that

I'm gonna win and they're gonna lose." She smiled. "I like that feeling."

"Well, sure," Buffy added, a bit of an edge to her voice. "It beats that dead feeling you get when they win and you lose." She piled French fries onto her plate.

"I don't let that kind of negative thinking in," Faith countered.

"Right . . ." Joyce said. "Right, *that* can get you hurt. Buffy can be awfully negative sometimes." She looked at Buffy. "See, honey, you've gotta fight that."

Buffy shot her an incredulous look. "Working on it."

Joyce saw that Faith's glass was empty. "Oh, Faith. Can I get you another soft drink?"

"Oh, you bet," the girl said gratefully.

As Joyce walked into the kitchen, she heard a short exchange between the girls.

"She's really cool, huh?" Faith commented.

"Best mom ever," Buffy agreed.

Joyce smiled to herself as she pulled a bottle of soda out of the refrigerator and began to refill Faith's glass. A moment later, Buffy walked in.

"I like this girl, Buffy," she told her daughter.

"She's very personable," Buffy said, icy sarcasm in her voice. "She gets along with my friends, my Watcher, my mom." She leaned back and glanced into the dining room, where Faith was apparently filching from her plate. "Look, now she's getting along with my fries."

"Now, Buffy—"

"Plus at school today she was making eyes at *my* not-boyfriend. This is creepy."

Joyce frowned. "Does anybody else think Faith is creepy?"

Buffy offered a tiny pout. "No. But I'm the one getting Single-White-Femaled here."

Another pop culture reference. A habit of her daughter's, but Joyce was relieved that at least this time it was about a movie she'd actually seen.

"It's probably good you were an only child," Joyce chided her.

"Mom, I'm just getting my life back," Buffy argued. "I'm not looking to go halfsies on it."

"Well, there are some things I'd be happy to see you share. Like the slaying. I mean, two of you fighting is safer than one, right?"

"I guess," Buffy conceded.

"Unless," Joyce went on, an idea beginning to form in her mind. "I mean, you heard her. She loves the slaying. Couldn't she take over for you?"

"Mom, no one can take over for me."

"But you're going to college next year. I think it would great if—"

Buffy glanced away. "Mom, the only way you get a new Slayer is when the old Slayer dies."

The words hit Joyce hard. Her mind reeled as she tried to make sense of them, put them in context. Her eyes widened as she stared at her daughter.

"But then that means you—" Shock turned to a bit of pique. "When did you die? You never *told* me you died."

"It was just for a few minutes," Buffy reasoned.

"Oh, I hate this," Joyce said, pacing the kitchen. "I hate your life."

"Mom—"

"I know you didn't choose this. I know it chose you. I have tried to march in the Slayer Pride Parade, but . . ." Her heart broke as she looked at her daughter. "I don't want you to die."

Buffy wrapped her arms around her mother and Joyce held on tight.

"I'm not going to die," Buffy promised. "I know how to do my job. Besides, like you said, I've got help now."

They looked out into the dining room to see Faith eating from one of the serving bowls.

"I've got all the help I can stand," Buffy sighed.

Hours after dark, when the streets were far too quiet and the breeze rustling a trash bag might turn out to be a creature of darkness, Buffy and Faith patrolled a particularly unpleasant area filled with warehouses and businesses long since closed for the night.

"Didn't we do this street already?" Faith asked, glancing around.

"Funny thing about vamps. They'll hit a street even after you've been there. It's like they have no manners." Though she was distracted by the tension she felt with Faith, Buffy stayed on alert, peering into every shadow they passed.

"Well," Faith said idly, "you've been doing this the longest."

"I have," Buffy agreed.

"Yeah, maybe a little too long."

"Excuse me?" Buffy snapped, rounding on her. "What's that supposed to mean?"

"Nothing." Faith kept walking.

"You got a problem?" Buffy demanded, keeping pace with her.

"I'm five by five, B. Livin' large. Actually wondering about *your* problem."

"Well, I may not sleep in the nude or rassle alligators—"

"Maybe it's time you started," Faith told her as they glanced around for vampires. " 'Cause obviously something in your bottle needs uncorking. What is it, the Angel thing?"

Buffy froze and stared at her. "What do you know about Angel?"

"Just what your friends tell me. Big love, big loss. You oughta deal and move on, but you're not."

Fuming, Buffy stepped in closer to her. "I got an idea. How 'bout from now on we don't hear from you on Angel, or anything else in my life? Which, by the way, is *my* life."

Faith cocked her head back and cast a challenging glance at Buffy. "What are you getting so strung out for, B?"

Buffy's nostrils flared with anger. "Why are your lips still moving, *F?*"

"Did I just hear a threat?"

"Would you like to?"

Faith smiled. "Wow. You think you can take me?"

"Yeah," Buffy said confidently.

Then she spotted a quartet of nasty-looking vampires rushing up from behind Faith.

"I just hope they can't!" she finished.

Shoving Faith out of the way, Buffy knocked the first vampire to reach her off his feet with a single, swift blow to the gut. A second was upon her immediately and she battered him with a flurry of punches, then spun him around hard, sending him reeling.

Faith was on her feet in an instant. She slammed a trash can down over the head of the third one.

The first one Buffy had struck attacked again, but she drove him to the ground and punched a stake through his heart. He exploded into a cloud of dust even as the other grabbed her from behind and hurled her against a fence. Buffy leaped up and as he rushed toward her, she snapped a hard side kick up at him, the power of which knocked him back onto the metal top of a Dumpster.

Faith traded blows with the fourth one nearby. The vampire got in a solid punch, but Faith shook it off easily. "My dead mother hits harder than that," she snarled at him as she flung him to the ground.

Faith leaped on top of the vampire and began to pummel him with blow after savage blow.

The one Faith had used the garbage can on was free,

and Buffy now had two vampires to deal with. She flipped one hard onto the ground, then glared at the other Slayer.

"Faith, stake him already and give me a hand!" she snapped.

But Faith just kept punching, her fist splitting the skin on the vampire's face and drawing blood. Before Buffy could shout at her again, she was surprised from the side by one of the other vamps. Buffy was dragged to the ground, pushed onto her face, and in a heartbeat they were behind her, and she was vulnerable.

"Yeah, this is me, you undead bastard!" Faith cried out in fury that sounded almost like she was in pain.

Meanwhile, Buffy really was in pain. The vampires were holding her down, and one of them lowered its fangs toward the back of her neck.

"For Kakistos we live," the other snarled. "For Kakistos, you die!"

A broken board was just inches beyond Buffy's reach. Impossible, frustrating inches.

"Faith!" she shouted.

But Faith was lost in the violence, lost in the blood on her fist and the pain she was inflicting on the vampire beneath her. Help was not coming. Buffy could not reach the splintered board, and she felt a spatter of cold saliva on the back of her neck as the vampire spread wide its jaws.

CHAPTER 3

I'm not gonna die.

With a burst of strength that surprised even her, Buffy dragged herself forward the last few inches to the shattered length of wood that lay on the pavement in front of her. Her fingers gripped it, and she used it to bat away the vampire that had hovered over her neck, savoring the anticipation of her blood.

Not tonight, she thought. *And not you.*

The wood struck its skull with a satisfying crack, driving the thing back and away from her. Now that she had some leverage, Buffy bucked the other one away, sprang to her feet, and easily dusted first one, then the other.

Furious at Faith, she turned to see that the other Slayer, who had gotten the best of the last vampire nearly a full minute earlier, was still hammering away with her fist at its face, pounding its flesh into a ragged mess.

"You! Can't! Touch! Me!" Faith sneered at the vamp, punctuating each word with another blow.

Mind reeling at the sight, and deeply troubled, Buffy

tore Faith off the vampire and quickly staked it. Dust swirled away in a light breeze that swept across the pavement.

Buffy spun and glared at Faith. "What is wrong with you?"

Faith winced, frowned at her. "What are you talking about?"

"I'm talking about you living large on that vampire," Buffy snapped.

"Gee, if doing violence to vampires upsets you, I think you're in the wrong line of work." Faith was cocky, almost sneering.

"Yeah, and maybe you like it a little too much."

Suddenly Faith's attitude shifted. From cocky, she became angry. "I was getting the job done."

"The job," Buffy said sternly, "is to slay demons. Not beat them to a bloody pulp while their friends corner me."

Faith crossed her arms, lips pursed. "I thought you could handle yourself."

Then she shrugged and walked off, leaving Buffy to stare after her in anger and astonishment.

In school the following morning, Buffy related the previous night's events to Giles, who had a stack of books under one arm and a cup of tea in the other. Much to her chagrin, the Watcher did not seem nearly as disturbed by Faith's actions as she was.

"What you must realize, Buffy, is that you and Faith have totally different temperaments," Giles explained, as the two of them strolled side by side down the school corridor.

Buffy shot him a look. "Yeah, and mine's the sane one. Girl's not playing with a full deck, Giles. She has almost no deck. She has a three."

"You said yourself that she killed one of them," he reminded her. "She's just a plucky fighter who got a little carried away. Which is natural. She's focused on the slaying. She doesn't have a whole other life here, as you do."

"She doesn't need another life," Buffy noted, an edge in her voice. "She has mine."

"I think you're being a little—"

"No, I'm being a lot," Buffy interrupted. She sighed. "I know that. But she nearly got us both killed. The girl needs help."

Giles took a sip of his tea and slowed just a bit. "I'll see if I can reach her Watcher at the retreat. They're . . ." He glanced at his watch, nearly spilling his tea in the process. ". . . eight hours ahead now." His eyes grew distant. "Yes, they're probably sitting down to a nightcap. I wonder if they still kayak. I used to love a good kayak. You see, they don't even consider—"

Buffy stared at him.

"Sorry, I digress," the Watcher murmured. "The vampires that attacked you. Can you furnish me with some details that might help me trace their lineage? Ancient or modern dress? Amulets? Cultish tattoos?"

He took another sip from his cup.

"No tats. Crappy dressers," Buffy thought about it for a moment. "Oh. The one that nearly bit me mentioned something about kissing toast. He lived for kissing toast."

Giles paused and turned to her. "You mean Kakistos?"

"Or maybe it was taquitos. Maybe he lived for taquitos."

Then she noticed the alarmed expression on the Watcher's face.

"Kakistos," he said, his tone unusually grave, even for Giles, before he rushed into the library.

Buffy raised an eyebrow. "Is that bad?"

When she followed him into the library, Giles was moving around like a man with a mission. He went into his interior office to retrieve a book.

"Kakistos is Greek," he explained urgently. "It means

the worst of the worst. It's also the name of a vampire so old that his hands and feet are cloven."

He brought the book to the checkout counter and began to riffle through pages, obviously searching for some kind of reference on Kakistos. Buffy frowned as she watched him, thoughts clicking into place in her head like pieces of a puzzle.

"Now, this guy shows up two days ago, right?" Buffy ventured. "Right around the time my bestest new little sister makes the scene."

Giles looked up from the book, a thoughtful expression on his face. "You think he and Faith are connected."

Buffy leaned on the counter. "Giles, there are two things that I don't believe in: coincidence and leprechauns."

"Now Buffy, it's entirely possible that they both arrived here by chance simultaneously."

"Okay," she replied reluctantly. "But I was right about the leprechauns?"

"As far as I know."

"Good." She nodded to herself. "Okay, you get England on the phone. I'm gonna talk to Faith, see if khaki-trousers—"

"Kakistos," Giles corrected.

"Kakistos . . . rings a bell. Or an alarm."

As Giles had said, it was entirely possible that all of the things that had been happening were nothing more than coincidence. But a nagging feeling in the back of Buffy's mind told her it was more than that. She felt driven to figure it all out as soon as possible, to take action. With that purpose pushing her on, she pushed out of the library and marched down the hallway, intent upon finding Faith.

She almost didn't notice Scott until he was right up beside her.

"Hi."

"Scott . . ."

"How are you?" he asked, a bit of nervousness in his voice.

"Uh, okay. Y'know, I gotta—"

"I know, be somewhere else, right? Think of this as my last-ditch effort. I realize that one more is going to qualify as stalking. I've given a lot of thought—some might say too much thought—to . . . to how I might be a part of your life. It begins with conversation. We all know this. Maybe over a cup of coffee, or maybe at the Buster Keaton festival playing on State Street all this weekend."

For a moment, Buffy could not think of a thing to say. Willow had been right about Scott, he *was* charm. A sweeter, nicer invitation she did not know if she had ever heard.

"You know," she said, with a tiny nod and a half-smile, "come to think of it, I don't think I've given a fair chance to . . . Buster Keaton. I . . . like what I've seen of him so far. I think it might be time to see a little more."

Scott's smile reached his eyes, which sparkled with delight. "Keaton is key," he said happily. "Oh, um, I got you a little present." He reached into his pocket and pulled out a small white box. "A guy in the retro shop said that it represents friendship. That's something I would very much like to have with you."

Scott handed her the box, and Buffy looked at it warily. She opened it. Inside was a claddagh ring, almost identical to the one Angel had given her, the one that had meant so much, the one that reminded her of the love she had been forced to betray, to destroy.

"You like?" Scott asked hopefully.

Buffy recoiled as though physically wounded, dropping the ring and box to the ground. "I can't," she said, shaking her head. "I can't do this."

Coming down the hall, Giles witnessed her distress, and walked quickly over to where she and Scott stood.

Scott knelt to retrieve the ring and the box, then looked at Buffy sadly.

"Okay," he said. "I get the message."

He walked off, leaving her standing there staring at the floor.

"Are you all right?" Giles reached out to comfort her but Buffy flinched and drew away from him.

Eyes wet with unfallen tears, Buffy looked up at him. "Oh, Giles. Hi. Yeah, I'm fine. Did you reach the retreat?"

Grimly, he nodded. "Yes, I did."

"What did her Watcher say?"

"Her Watcher is dead."

In the stale-smelling motel room she had found upon first arriving in town, Faith and the motel manager faced off across the stained carpet. The guy was an unshaven, stinky mess in a white tee shirt, but he seemed to have a decent heart. Or, at least, a soft spot for wild girls.

"Room's eighteen dollars a day. That's every day," he reminded her.

"Yeah, I know," she told him. "I'll get it to you by to-morrow, I swear."

He sighed. "It's not like I own the place."

Faith smiled coquettishly. "Bet you will someday."

The manager rolled his eyes, surrendering to her. "Not if I listen to broads like you."

He turned to go just as Buffy stepped through the open door. When he spotted her, he gave Faith a hard look.

"Roommates are extra."

"I'm just visiting," Buffy assured him.

The manager glanced at Faith again, but she only shrugged. He walked out and Buffy shut the door behind him. Faith did not miss the sad, dark expression on her face.

"What brings you to the poor side of town?" she asked.

"Cloven guy," Buffy said, fixing her with a piercing stare. "Goes by the name Kakistos."

Faith felt her pulse begin to race, her heart beating faster even as her eyes went wide and a sick chill roiled in her gut. "What do you know about Kakistos?"

"That he's here."

Faith felt as if the wind had been knocked out of her. Panic surged through, and all the fear she had buried so deep came rushing back out as if it had been just waiting for this opportunity. And she knew it had.

Buffy must have noticed the expression on her face. "We're not happy to see old friends, are we?"

The question barely registered. Faith was already glancing around the room, calculating how long it would take her to grab her few things, and how far away she could be by morning.

"What'd he do to you?" Buffy asked.

"It's what I did to him," Faith admitted. Then she grabbed her bag and started to pack.

"And what was that?"

Scrambling, shoving stuff into her bag, Faith ignored her. But Buffy would not be put off.

"Faith, you came here for a reason. I can help."

"You can mind your own business. I'm the one who can handle this," Faith replied.

"Yeah, you're a real badass when it comes to packing. What was that you said about my problem? You gotta deal and move on? Well, you have the moving-on part right here. What about dealing? Is that just something you're gonna dump on me?"

Frenzied now, trying to keep the panic out of her voice, Faith rounded on Buffy. "You don't know me. You don't know what I've been through. I'll take care of this, all right?"

Her bag packed, she started for the door.

"Like you took care of your Watcher?" Buffy prodded.

Faith froze, despair stopping her in her tracks. The Slayer's words were like a dagger in her heart. Slowly, feeling helpless, she turned to stare at Buffy.

"He killed her, didn't he?"

Faith's response was little more than a whisper. "They don't have a word for what he did to her."

A knock came at the door. Faith started, and swore under her breath. She put her eye to the peephole. The manager was standing on the doorstep again.

"What now?" she muttered in frustration.

"Faith, you run, he runs after you," Buffy warned.

"That's where the head start comes in handy," Faith told her.

She opened the door.

Kakistos stood outside with several of his vampire lackeys. He held the manager by the back of the neck with one powerful hand. At the sight of his horrible visage, the scarred countenance that had haunted her day and night, all the breath went out of her. Faith stared at him, eyes wide with horror.

The manager slumped to the ground, dead.

Then Kakistos spoke her name.

CHAPTER 4

Faith was frozen. Maybe she still thought Kakistos couldn't come in. Maybe she was just afraid. But when the scarred vampire reached in and gripped her by the throat, choking her, beginning to crush her windpipe, Faith barely fought back.

Buffy lunged for the door and shoved it with all her extraordinary strength. Finally, Faith beat at Kakistos's grip and freed herself. Again Buffy slammed the door on his arm and Kakistos withdrew. Desperate, she turned the flimsy lock and slid the chain across the door.

"No," Faith muttered, almost shuddering with fear. "*No.*"

"It's okay," Buffy told her. "I just bought us a little—"

Kakistos punched a huge, cloven fist through the door, sending shards of wood flying.

"—time."

Faith screamed now. "No!" she cried, as though she could deny it all, pretend it wasn't happening. She began to collapse onto the filthy carpet. *This isn't happening!*

"Scream later!" Buffy snapped at her as Kakistos battered at the door. "Escape now!" Her tone roused Faith from the dark images in her head. Images of her Watcher.

Buffy raced across the room, picked up a chair and hurled it through the window. Glass showered out into the alley below. Even as Kakistos kicked the door off its hinges, Faith leaped out the window and Buffy followed an eyeblink later.

Together they ran, side by side, down the alley to a T-junction. There were warehouses and other businesses all around. Buffy did not hesitate. She turned left at the junction, aiming for the street and more populated areas. One glimpse out the door had told them that Kakistos had a great many followers with him.

A backward glance told the girls that if they did not find a place to hide momentarily, the fight was going to happen whether she wanted it to or not. Kakistos himself was giving chase, along with at least four other vampires.

Off to her left, Buffy spotted an opening in a boarded-up window.

"Here," she whispered harshly. She crashed through the wood and glass and rolled onto the floor. Faith was right behind her, functioning on pure Slayer reflex. When she sprang to her feet, she saw Kakistos run by outside the window. It was a miracle, but he had not heard the smashing glass.

"We're okay," Buffy said. She gazed at Faith intensely. "What happened?"

Faith only shook her head, obviously reluctant to speak.

"Faith," Buffy urged her.

"I . . . I was there," the other Slayer said at last. "When he killed my Watcher. I saw what he did to her. What he was gonna do to me. I tried to stop him but I couldn't. And I ran . . . *and he followed*."

"Faith, first rule of slaying: don't die. You did the right

thing, okay? You didn't die. Now you do the math. One of him, two of us.

"*What the —?*"

Buffy was trying to comfort her. Then she saw that Faith's terrified gaze was not drifting, but was instead locked onto a spot just over Buffy's shoulder.

"No," Faith muttered, shaking her head.

Slowly, Buffy turned. In the corner were the corpses of three delivery men.

"This is his place," Faith gasped.

"He drove us here." Buffy glanced around, alert now.

A long-haired female vamp appeared suddenly in the shattered window. Buffy and Faith turned and ran the length of the abandoned firehouse, even as two more vampires erupted from the shadows and lunged for them. With a single, swift motion, Buffy kicked an enormous plastic bucket at one of them. The other two converged. She leaped and kicked the one in front of her, then spun and kicked the other in the face, knocking both down.

Faith stood immobile.

Even as Buffy continued to fight them off, Kakistos emerged from the shadows and stalked across the firehouse toward Faith. Distantly, Faith heard Buffy call her name, but she only stood and stared at Kakistos, her memory of what he had done more powerful than the urge to protect herself.

"Don't die!" Buffy shouted at her.

Buffy tossed a tire iron and Faith automatically snatched it from the air. At last, instinct took over and Faith tried to protect herself. *Don't die!* Terror in her eyes, she swung at Kakistos. He struck her in the face hard enough to drive her backward into a wooden column with such force that the support beam broke and slammed to the floor next to her.

Buffy tried to go to Faith's aid, but she was grabbed from behind. She heard Faith's whimpers of pain as Kakistos beat her—almost the same way she had beaten that vampire the night before—but Buffy could not help her. Not yet.

Don't die, Buffy thought, and the words were for Faith, and for herself.

A flurry of blows and she drove the vampire down. She punched the stake through its heart and it dusted. When Buffy turned she saw that Kakistos had Faith by the throat, choking her. He threw her to the ground, then prepared for the final attack. Buffy ran at him, brutalized him with a combination of punches and kicks.

He barely flinched.

Trick watched the battle with growing unease. He stepped up beside another of Kakistos's people, a blond vampire woman whose name he always had trouble recalling. Not that it mattered. He liked the way she looked. It would be a shame if she died. Even more of a shame if he ended up dust himself.

"We don't do something, the master could get killed," he said.

The girl glanced at him, their eyes communicating an unspoken agreement.

"Well, our prayers are with him," Trick said idly. "There's a reason these vengeance crusades are out of style. You see the modern vampire. You see the big picture."

Together, the two vampires turned to go.

Kakistos was on his own.

Buffy slammed the stake at Kakistos's chest. His powerful hand clasped her wrist, stopping her. She tried to hit him again, but he batted her into the concrete wall.

"Looks like you need a bigger stake, Slayer," Kakistos taunted her. Then he began to laugh, deep and raspy. He had the upper hand and he knew it.

Movement off to her left drew Buffy's glance. She turned in time to see Faith pick up the huge wooden column that had snapped off in her fight with Kakistos. Faith hefted the thing over her shoulder with both hands and lunged at Kakistos.

The vampire was still laughing as the enormous shaft of wood pierced his chest. He grunted in pain and then stared down at it for a second before exploding into a ball of cinder and ash.

Stunned, Buffy stared open-mouthed at the place where Kakistos had been. Winded, breathing hard, she and Faith moved closer to one another, glancing around to see if it was truly over.

"You hungry?" Buffy asked.

Faith nodded. "Starved."

The next morning, Buffy stood in the library with Willow as Giles finished a phone call in his office. While Giles was otherwise engaged, Buffy caught Willow up on everything that had happened the day before. But as the Watcher's conversation went on, she and Willow became distracted by the seriousness of his tone and their own talking stopped.

At length he hung up and came out into the library.

"The Council has approved our request. Faith is to stay here indefinitely," he told Buffy. "And I'm to look after you both until a new Watcher is assigned."

"Good," Buffy said thoughtfully. "She really came through in the end. She had a lot to deal with, but she did it. She got it behind her."

Even as she spoke, she felt the import of her words. Faith had been forced to confront her past. To deal with it and move on. How could Buffy herself do any less?

Giles nodded. "I'm glad to hear it."

Deal with it and move on, she thought to herself.

"Angel was cured," she said suddenly, her eyes growing moist.

Willow stared at her, stunned.

Grave concern etched on his face, Giles studied her closely. "I'm sorry?"

"When I killed him. Angel was cured." Buffy glanced at Willow. "Your spell worked at the last minute, Will." Her eyes went to Giles again. "I was about to take him out and, um, something went through him and he was Angel again. He didn't remember anything . . . that he'd done. He just held me. But it was . . . it was too late and I had to. So I told him that I loved him. And I kissed him. And I killed him."

The pain blossomed anew in her heart. Her eyes stung. And yet, somehow, speaking the words, putting them in the past tense . . . it helped.

"I don't know if that helps with your spell or not, Giles."

"Yes," he said softly. "I believe it will."

"I'm sorry," Willow offered, her eyes reflecting Buffy's own pain.

"It's okay. I've been holding onto that for so long. It felt good to get it out," Buffy told her. And it was true. "I'll see you guys later."

Willow watched her best friend leave the library, aching with sympathy for Buffy. Yet her shock at what Buffy had gone through was tempered by her knowledge that she had begun to move past that horror and pain. Willow only wished there was something more that she could do.

And then she realized there was.

"Giles," Willow said quickly, "I know you don't like me playing with mystical forces, but I can really help with this binding spell."

A resigned expression on his face, Giles did not even turn to her as he replied. "There is no spell."

It took a moment, as he walked away, for Willow to realize what he meant. All along, Giles had been prodding Buffy for information about the final moments of her battle with Angel and Acathla, claiming it was for this binding spell. But the spell was only a ruse. He had invented it merely to get Buffy to open up, to confront her pain, to help her in his own way to mend her broken heart.

Sometimes Willow forgot what an amazing man the Watcher was.

She doubted she would ever do so again.

Buffy waited in the hall for Scott to get out of class. When she saw him emerge, slinging his pack onto his back, she almost didn't approach him. Almost.

"Scott."

"Oh. Hello," he said hesitantly.

"Hi. Um, I was waiting for you to get out of class."

"Why?"

Buffy smiled, paused only for a moment, and then forged recklessly ahead. "Um, there was someone. A while ago. The ring sort of confused me. But I liked what you said about friendship. I liked it a lot. And Buster Keaton is big fun. And I'm capable of big fun, even though there's no earthly way you could possibly know that about me. Wow, if I'd known I was gonna go on this long I probably would've brought some water."

A breath. Scott didn't look convinced.

"What I'm trying to say is if you would still like to go the film festival—and I would understand if you didn't— I'd pretty much love to go with you."

Scott blew out a breath, glanced around, not meeting her eyes. "Umm, I don't know, Buffy. I'm really going to have to think about this."

Then he turned to walk away. Buffy tried to fight the disappointment she felt. It was her fault, after all. She couldn't expect him to just put her bizarre behavior behind him. She had just about convinced herself of that when Scott turned around and came back.

"Okay, you know what? I thought about it and I'm in. When do you want to go?"

Buffy smiled. "Well, I have one thing that I have to do tonight. Then I'm good."

Scott nodded. "Good."

For a long time, Buffy had stayed away from the mansion, the enormous old home where Angel had once lived. Where he had died. Where she had killed him. It was a beautiful place, but cold without him, and haunted by her memories. Horrors had taken place here. During the time when Angel's soul had been taken from him and only the demon within him remained, he had perpetrated many hideous acts within these walls.

She moved through the cold rooms until she came to the very spot where she had impaled him upon a ritual sword. Through the demon Acathla, a portal had been opened to Hell. The only way for her to close it was with Angel's blood. She had run him through with the blade, given him the slightest push, and the portal had drawn him in.

With his blood, it was resealed. It closed up again with him on the other side.

She had slain the one she loved and sent him to Hell.

But it was over now. There had been no other choice, and she knew that. It was time to move on.

In her hand, she clutched the claddagh ring tightly. She knelt down on the stone floor where he had died.

"Good-bye," she whispered.

Gently, she placed the ring on the cold ground, rose, and turned to walk slowly from the place that had been Angel's home.

Her ghosts were at rest.

* * *

In the darkness, a glow.

On the stone floor, the ring shimmered with light. It began to dance as the ground rumbled beneath it. A hum built as otherworldly energy surged and the rumble grew louder.

A flash of brilliance like lightning sliced the air inside that cold room, a tear in the barriers between worlds opened, and the naked form of a man tumbled out of nothing to slam painfully to the floor, only inches from where Buffy had laid her ring.

Like a wild animal released from its cage, Angel glared about at his surroundings. He had been in Hell for what seemed like an eternity. His mind was not what it once had been. He was mad, now.

Or nearly.

Getting Out

Get out more.

It had been Giles's suggestion, and Faith was starting to think it had been a good one. For the first couple of weeks after she'd dusted Kakistos, Faith had spent the time while Buffy and her friends were in school back at her skanky motel room watching television or sleeping. But there was only so much *Jerry Springer* she could take before she started feeling like just as much of a loser as the guests on the talk shows.

No way was she going to let herself sink that low.

Though he and Buffy didn't push Faith to talk much about the death of her Watcher and the whole thing with Kakistos—for which she was grateful—Giles often asked her how she was doing. How she was adjusting.

"Five by five," she'd always say.

Only a week or so ago, she'd been a little more honest than usual. Giles had a way of bringing that out in her. He was a dweeb, yeah, but like a lot of the other people in Buffy's life, he stirred ideas in Faith's head about what it would be like to have friends and family. Sometimes it made her hope, and she'd push that hope away. Better not to think about it. Better to just go with the flow, not expect too much from people.

Start expecting things from people and they'd always let you down: Faith had been taught that lesson from birth.

But that one afternoon she was just too tired to pretend. So when Giles asked how she had been doing, she told the truth.

"Bored to freakin' tears. You guys have, like, lives to deal with. Me, I'm just about the Slaying. Makes the days go by kinda slow."

Giles had taken off his glasses and started cleaning them—which he did often enough for it to be called a habit—and then smiled. "Perhaps you ought to get out more. Learn a bit more about your new hometown. Sunnydale does have things to offer other than demons trying to kill you."

It had taken her days before she acted on the advice, but now Faith was glad she had.

In jeans and a tiny top with spaghetti straps—all black—she wandered downtown Sunnydale, taking it all in. The Sun Cinema marquee was lit up, and it made her think about how long it had been since she'd even been to the movies. Since Boston, she realized, and that seemed like a very, very long time ago.

Women pushed baby strollers along the sidewalk. Businessmen in power suits talked on cell phones where they were seated at tables at a patio café. A police car rolled on by and the brake lights didn't even come on, though Faith tensed a bit at the sight of it. A guy and girl in differently-styled U.C. Sunnydale sweatshirts went by hand in hand.

On the corner, an old man who wore a sweater despite the warmth of the day watched her as she approached. He had a golden retriever on a leash and gave the dog plenty of leeway to sniff around the bottom of a lamppost.

"Beautiful day," the old man rasped, smiling pleasantly.

Faith stared at him, trying to figure out if the guy was a panhandler or some pervert or even a demon setting her up. His smile faltered and he looked at her oddly and dragged the dog away, and only then did she realize a startling truth.

He was the real thing. Sweet old guy walking his dog, saying good morning. The real thing.

Weird, she thought.

But she liked it. As she kept on walking, she took in more of the town, and wondered what it would be like if she could ever really come to think of the place as home. *It'd be something,* she thought, *to think of Sunnydale as home.* There had been a time when she wondered if she would ever be able to use that word again.

As she passed the Espresso Pump, Faith paused and glanced through the long windows at a quartet of thirty-something women engaged in an animated conversation. Their hands flew as they gossiped and laughed between sips of mochaccino, or whatever they were drinking.

They were like aliens to Faith. Friends, almost sisters to each other, people who could be that free and open together. That trusting.

Weird, she thought again.

Faith doubted if she could ever be that open with anyone. Even though Buffy and her friends had been pretty good about including her, and Giles had been pretty cool to her, she wondered if she could ever think of them as *her* friends.

For a while, she had started to think she and Buffy really had an understanding. But then, Buffy had been acting sort of peculiar lately.

Faith's upper lip curled just a bit as she turned away from the window, trying to put the women at the table out of her mind. Giles had been right that she needed to get out more, and Sunnydale was a nice little town.

But it wasn't home.

Whatever that was.

Faith would not allow herself to hope that it ever would be.

REVELATIONS

CHAPTER 1

Willow hated secrets. Well, okay, there was nothing wrong with happy secrets, particularly someone else's. But at the moment, she was thinking secrets pretty much stink.

Dingoes Ate My Baby jammed on the stage in the Bronze. The place was packed to capacity—maybe over capacity—and Willow sat with Xander and Cordelia watching the show. Onstage, under the multicolored lights, Oz hit all the right chords. He was really getting pretty good, despite his self-deprecating attitude about his playing.

He glanced up, caught Willow's eye, and smiled sweetly, knowingly. A shiver went through her. Her boyfriend—and he was the most wonderful guy she had ever known.

Yet now she was having feelings for Xander.

Cordelia laughed about something and Xander smiled. Then he glanced at Willow and looked quickly away. The guilt crackled between them like electricity.

What's wrong with us? Willow thought. *We've both got someone we really love. What are we doing?* The truth was that she didn't know. Right now she could not imagine making such a huge and stupid mistake as to share any kind of intimacy with Xander, even a kiss, but then she recalled the way she'd been feeling recently anytime they were alone together. It was like something came over her.

He had been her best friend almost all her life. For years, she had had a deep crush on him, but he had never paid that kind of attention to her. Then when she finally found Oz, found love . . . it was enough to make her hate Xander. But she could never do that. And he wasn't the only one at fault, in any case.

The guilt was terrible.

Willow focused on Oz, onstage, and smiled lovingly at him. Dingoes finished their set and he slipped off his guitar, ignored the adoring groupies, and sauntered over to the table.

"Oz! Hey," she said. "Have a seat. Except, we don't have any seats."

He glanced at the packed table. "It's okay. I'll just scrunch in."

He slid onto the chair with Willow, pushing her uncomfortably close to Xander, who moved away quickly.

Cordelia frowned. "Xander, why are you giving me a lap dance?"

"What? I just like you."

"And that's very beautiful," Willow said, a little too quickly. "I think it's great when two people like two people and want to be close to them instead of anyone else."

Xander nodded. "Hear, hear."

"Yeah, well put," Oz said. He pointed to Xander's soda cup. "Hey, can I snag a sip?"

"Sure," Willow

At precisely th   ne moment Xander said, "Yeah, you got it."

They reached fc the cup and their hands brushed against each other Xander flinched back as though he'd received an electric shock, knocking a drink tray from a waitress's hand and sending beverages flying. The crowd in the Bronze laughed and applauded his bumbling.

Not Willow, though. She gazed about nervously, wondering if anyone had an inkling about the reason for Xander's reaction.

"Thank you," Xander told his appreciative audience. "We're here through Saturday. Enjoy the veal."

As he sat back down, a profoundly embarrassed Cordelia leaned in toward them.

"Why are you guys so hyper?" she asked.

"Hey, speaking of people and things they do that aren't like usual, anyone notice Buffy acting sort of different?" Willow put in quickly, and awkwardly.

"Let's see," Xander replied, not really getting the hint. "Killing zombies, torching sewer monsters, and, um . . . no that's pretty much the same old Buffster."

"I just mean, y'know she's off by herself a lot more? And she's kind of distracted."

"Think maybe she has a new honey?" Cordelia inquired, ready for the gossip.

Willow frowned. "A boyfriend? Why wouldn't she tell us?"

Cordelia's eyebrows shot up. "Excuse me. When your last steady kills half the class and then your rebound guy sends you a dump-o-gram? It makes a girl shy."

It was true, Willow knew. Buffy had not had the best of luck with dating. Angel had turned evil and Buffy had been forced to kill him. And then she dated Scott Hope for a little while before he decided maybe things weren't right between them. It had to be tough.

"But we're the best of Buffy's bestest buds," Xander said, a bit petulantly. "She'd tell us."

Even as he said it, Buffy pushed through the gathered Bronzers and appeared behind him.

"Tell you what?"

"About your new boyfriend," Willow explained. "Who we made up. Unless we didn't."

Buffy gave them a dubious glance. "This was a topic of discussion?"

"Raised, but never discussed," Oz corrected.

"So," Cordelia prodded, "are you dating somebody or not?"

A tiny half-smile reached Buffy's lips. "Well, I wouldn't use the word dating. But I am going out with somebody. Tonight, as a matter of fact."

"Really? Who?" Willow asked, thrilled to hear it.

Buffy only smiled ironically as Faith bopped up to the table. The new Slayer greeted the group with a nod.

"What's up?" She turned to Buffy. "Hey, time to motorvate."

With a dead-serious expression, Buffy slipped an arm around the other Slayer. "Really, we're just good friends."

In the cemetery.

In action.

Faith wore a white tee under a black sweatshirt. Dark pants. Buffy's outfit was similar, though she had her sweatshirt zipped up the front and wore a black watch cap with the word "bomb" written across the front in glittery silver. Faith liked the hat. Totally made the outfit.

Back to back, the Slayers confronted a pair of brutal vampires who had had the audacity to think they could make it in Sunnydale without tasting stake. They were decent hand-to-hand fighters, actually, these two vamps. But Buffy and Faith together? Unbeatable.

We're a thing of beauty, Faith thought as she cracked the jaw of the vamp she was fighting.

Faith didn't have a best friend right now. But she was starting to remember what it was like. The last four weeks as they had patrolled together more and more, they had become a well-oiled team. They had also started to become friends.

Meanwhile, Rupert Giles, the man who was now Watcher to them both, sat on a marble bench nearby with a thermos of tea, a Styrofoam cup, and a pad upon which he took notes about their efficiency. His expression was a combination of boredom and amusement. Faith liked that about him.

The vamp Faith was fighting, a Woody Harrelson-looking dude, tried to kick her in the face. She flipped him over, then wailed on him a few times until he shifted direction. One more blow, and he slammed into the other vampire.

Faith glanced up. Buffy hit her opponent one more time. They had the two vamps back to back, and simultaneously, they each brought down their stakes. Both vampires were dust.

"Synchronized Slaying," Buffy said as the girls high-fived.

"New Olympic category," Faith observed.

Buffy looked at Giles. "What do you think?"

Before he could reply, a woman's voice came out of the shadows of the cemetery.

"Sloppy."

A thin, pale, but attractive woman in a power suit and pearls walked toward them. When she spoke, it was with a British accent.

"You telegraph punches, leave blind sides open and, for a school night slaying, you both take entirely too much time. Which one of you is Faith?"

"Depends," Faith told her, bristling. "Who the hell are you?"

The woman lifted her chin with an air of superiority. "Gwendolyn Post. Mrs. Your new Watcher."

CHAPTER 2

A short time later, both Slayers and Watchers had retreated to the Sunnydale High library. It was long after dark, of course, but Giles had a key. The library was sort of Slayer Central, a sanctuary, though tonight it seemed like that sanctuary had been invaded.

Mrs. Post sifted through Giles's oldest books as he, Buffy and Faith looked on.

"Look, I'm telling you, I don't need a new Watcher," Faith said emphatically. "No offense, lady, I just have this problem with authority figures. They end up kinda dead."

"Duly noted," Mrs. Post replied. "And fortunately, it's not up to you." She glanced at Giles. "Mr. Giles, where do you keep the rest of your books?"

"I'm sorry, the rest?"

"Yes. The actual library?"

Giles blinked, taken aback, and more than a bit miffed.

"Oh," the newly arrived Watcher sniffed. "I see."

"I assure you, Mrs. Post, this is the finest occult reference collection—"

"This side of the Atlantic, I'm sure," she interrupted. "Do you have Hume's *Paranormal Encyclopedia?*"

Giles grumbled.

"The Labyrinth Maps of Malta?"

He glanced down. "It's on order."

"Well, I suppose that you have Sir Robert Kane's *Twilight Compendium?*"

"Oh, yes," Giles said, relieved. He reached for the book. "Yes. Yes I do."

"Yes. Of course you do," Mrs. Post replied, her tone painfully condescending. She turned to the girls. "I have been sent by the Council for a very important reason. Faith needs a Watcher. I am to act in that capacity and report back."

Faith cocked her head to one side, all attitude. "Excuse me, Mary Poppins, you don't seem to be listening."

Frustrated, Giles nevertheless signaled her to be quiet. "Faith, if the Council feels you need closer observation, we will all, of course, cooperate."

"The Council wishes me to report on the entire situation here," Mrs. Post told him. "Including you."

Appalled, Giles stared at her.

"Academic probation's not so funny today, huh Giles?" Buffy quipped.

"The fact is, there is talk in the Council that you have become a bit too . . . American," Mrs. Post revealed.

"Me?" Giles asked, aghast.

"Him?" Buffy chimed in.

As if bored by the entire conversation, Mrs. Post went on. "A demon named Lagos is coming here, to the Hellmouth. Mr. Giles, an illustration of Lagos, if you please."

Still reeling, Giles fumbled for a book that would contain the requested illustration. After only a few moments, Mrs. Post cast him a dismissive glance.

"Perhaps later," she sniffed.

Giles fumed.

"Lagos seeks the Glove of Myhnegon. No record of this glove's full power exists. But we do know it is highly dangerous and must not fall into the hands of a demon. Lagos must be stopped."

In an attempt to cooperate, Giles nodded. "What do you propose?"

Disdainful, Mrs. Post glared down her nose at him. "Well, if it's not too radical a suggestion, I thought we might kill him. I suggest two Slayers at full strength for a coordinated hunt. We believe the glove to be buried in a tomb somewhere, so Lagos will be headed for the cemetery."

Furious, but no longer even attempting to hide his displeasure, Giles did not even look at her. "There *is* more than one in Sunnydale."

"I see. How many?"

"Twelve. Within the city limits."

"Well, we'll just have to take them one at a time. Anything in your books that might pinpoint the exact location of the tomb would be useful, but then, we cannot ask for miracles." Mrs. Post turned to the Slayers. "We'll begin tomorrow at sunset. Faith? With me, please."

Reluctantly, Faith rose and followed Mrs. Post out the library doors.

"Well," Giles sighed, when they were gone. "That was bracing."

"Interesting lady," Buffy said brightly. "Can I kill her?"

Giles considered the question for a moment. "I think the Council might frown upon that."

The following afternoon, Buffy and Angel practiced Tai Chi at his mansion on the outskirts of Sunnydale. Once, the place had represented only sorrow for her, but it was becoming a kind of sanctuary from the rest of the world. In that very place, Buffy had prevented the apocalypse by running Angel through with a sword and pushing him into a hellish vortex. It had been the only way to close that vortex, the only way to save the world. And it had happened at the precise moment when Willow had succeeded with the spell to give Angel his soul back, make him good again.

Somehow he had been returned to Earth, but they did not know by whom or for what purpose. At first Angel had been little more than an animal, a ravening beast, and Buffy had been forced to chain him in the mansion. But slowly he began to regain his senses, to recognize her, and then he was finally able to tell her what little he knew of his time in that dark, demon dimension. Though he had forgotten a great deal, he knew that he had been there for what seemed an eternity; many years instead of the months he had been absent from the mortal plane of existence.

Buffy still shuddered to recall Angel in that animal state. A savage murder in Sunnydale had coincided with his escape from her captivity, and she had briefly feared that he was responsible. Her relief to discover he was not still lingered.

They moved through the Tai Chi routine together. Angel had spent hours each day gliding through the positions, centering himself, pushing out the horrors of his time in the Hell. Becoming Angel again. With Buffy's help, he had found himself. Weeks had passed. Everything was as back to normal as it could ever get, considering what had gone before.

With all her heart, Buffy loved him, and she knew Angel felt the same. But they could never be intimate again. As part of the curse that made him different from other vampires, the spell that kept his human soul within him, there was a caveat. A moment of perfect happiness, a single moment, and he would lose his soul once more.

It had happened once and the demon inside him—freed from its constant struggle now that his human soul was gone—had gone on a killing spree. Giles's girlfriend, Jenny Calendar, had been one of his victims. Though he was himself again, Buffy knew that it would be no simple task for Giles and her friends to forget what he had done, no matter what the circumstances. It was difficult for her to forget, though she knew it was not truly Angel who had done it.

Better to meet with him here in secret.

To love him. To rejoice in his return, but never be able to share her happiness.

A secret. But, still, it was better than any alternative she could think of. She knew she should tell them all. They deserved to know. But she had been through so much of late, she wanted to hold this one good thing just for herself for a while.

His body moved so perfectly, lithely, and she mirrored his every move. He had changed since his return, become quieter and more contemplative, his eyes even more haunted than they had been before.

Angel slipped behind her, strong hands on hers, and helped her follow through the movements, guiding her. His arms wrapped around her and slowly, she turned. Their eyes met, their lips so close, and moving closer . . .

Buffy broke away. "I gotta go." She went to grab her bag, slipped it over her shoulder. "Big night for us Slayer types. People to see, demons to kill. Better hurry before somebody figures out what we're doing."

"What *are* we doing?" Angel asked as he slowly slipped his shirt on and began to button it.

"Training," Buffy said. She turned to face him. "And almost kissing. Sorry. It's just . . . old habit. Bad, bad habit, to be broken."

"It's hard," Angel said, his dark eyes boring into her.

"It's not hard," Buffy replied, the lie sounding hollow

even to her. "Cold turkey. The key to quitting." With the longing aching in her heart, she gazed at him. "You think they make a patch for this?"

"You have to go," Angel told her.

"I really do. I'm gonna try and vent a little hormonal angst by going out there and killing a Lagos, whatever that is."

She barely noticed the way Angel's eyes lit up at the mention of the name. "Lagos," he repeated.

"Some demon looking for some all-powerful thing-amabob and I've gotta stop him before he unleashes un-holy havoc and it's another Tuesday night in Sunnydale."

Angel stared off into the gray, shadowed corners of the room. "Be careful."

Later that night, after hours aiding Giles with his re-search, Willow and Xander looked in on silence as his frustration finally got the better of him.

"This is intolerable," he snapped, slamming a book closed and getting up from the study table. "There's not a word here about Lagos or the glove. We don't have time for this near-missing. Just find out all you can about the demon; its strengths, its weaknesses, its places of origin, and most importantly, what it plans to do with this blasted glove."

Xander blinked, taken aback. "Hey, you're not the Watcher of me."

"Then go home," Giles replied grimly. "But if you choose to stay, then work." He retreated to his interior of-fice.

Exhausted, Xander trudged up the stairs to the raised rear level of the library, where most of the books were kept. At the top of the steps, Willow was waiting for him.

"Uggh," she sighed. "It's late. I'm tired. What does he want from us anyway?"

"The number of a qualified surgeon to remove the

British flag up his butt," Xander grumbled, as they moved into the stacks together.

They reached the spot at the back where they had spread out reference books, and sat down. Books in hand, they leaned against a shelf of books and started to research again. Willow groaned and leaned forward, rubbing her temples.

"My eyes are so blurry," she murmured.

Xander paused in his reading and looked at her. She seemed even more exhausted than he felt. He set the book down and reached out to gently massage her temples.

"Mmm," she moaned. Then, suddenly, she stiffened. "Stop."

"Right," he said softly, fingers still moving on her temples. "Stop means no. And no means no. So . . ." He withdrew his hands. "Stop."

He reached for the book again. Willow opened her eyes and turned to gaze at him. Then she kissed him. He didn't fight it. The kiss was deep and filled with longing and sparks went off in Xander's head.

"Willow. Xander."

They sprang apart, and looked up in horror as Giles wandered to a shelf nearby, his nose in another book. They stood up quickly, but there was no way to tell if he had seen them kissing. Willow clapped a hand over her mouth, panicked.

"You can stop your studying. I've got what I need."

Xander struggled to form a reply, but for a moment, he was speechless.

"What . . . what've you got?" he finally managed.

He turned to them. "A probable location of the Glove of Myhnegon. It's housed in the Von Hauptman family crypt."

"Yeah, that's the big one over at the Restfield Cemetery," Xander said quickly.

"That's great, Giles," Willow chimed in. "How'd you find it?"

He cast them a withering glance. "I looked."

"Where's Buffy at?" Xander asked.

"I'm not sure," Giles replied without looking up from his book.

"Well, I'll go check out this crypt. Tell her heads up if she stops by," Xander said nervously.

"Yes, by all means go." Giles paid no attention as Xander headed off through the stacks.

"I can keep studying," Willow offered. "I think we're on the verge of a big Lagos breakthrough."

As Xander went down the stairs, he heard Giles reply.

"No. I'd say we're done."

Cemetery by cemetery, Buffy and Faith had made their way through Sunnydale. Along the way, they'd gotten to talk even more than usual, and Faith had felt herself relaxing. Buffy had seemed a little distracted lately, but tonight everything was of the good.

Faith kept glancing at the other Slayer out of the corner of her eye. Maybe they weren't best friends, maybe they'd never be sisters, but they did connect. Faith felt it. It was an extraordinary thing for her to have someone with whom she shared so much, had so much in common. Almost all her life she'd been essentially alone. Even when she became a Slayer, that only set her further apart from other people. But it was different with Buffy. They were two of a kind. Normal humans could never have understood what Faith felt inside, but she really thought Buffy could.

They strode side by side through downtown Sunnydale.

"Ronnie, deadbeat. Steve, klepto. Kenny, *drummer*," Faith said, particularly scornful about Kenny's status as a musician. "Eventually I had to accept my destiny as a loser magnet. Now it's just get some, get gone. You can't trust guys."

"You can trust some guys," Buffy argued. "Really, I've read about them."

"So what about you?"

"You mean, like, me and guys, me? Not much to tell these days."

"Yeah, but you've gotta have stories," Faith urged. She wanted Buffy to open up to her more, to share what she really felt. "I mean, I've had my share of losers, but you boinked the undead. What was that like?"

Buffy blinked, a troubled expression passing like a cloud across her face. "Life with Angel . . . *was* . . . complicated," she said. "It's still a little hard for me to talk about."

"Try." Faith smiled.

Buffy seemed to bristle a little. "Look, Faith, all of the Angel issues are still kinda with me, so if you don't mind, I'd rather not."

Faith's smile faded. She was hurt. All of the things she had been thinking about Buffy, about what they shared, seemed like wishful thinking all of a sudden.

"Yeah, whatever. You know what, we're oh for six tonight. Why don't we just blow this off?"

"I am kinda beat," Buffy admitted. "But Shady Hill's pretty close."

"I'll swing through it," Faith offered. "It's on my way home."

"Alone?" Buffy asked. "I don't know if—"

"I got Miss Priss on my back now," Faith reminded her. "I don't need another baby-sitter. I'll holler if I'm having any fun."

"Okay," Buffy relented.

Faith nodded once. "Later."

She had already put Buffy out of her mind by the time she got to Shady Hill. That was the way she always dealt with things that hurt. Not that she would ever admit that the other girl's gentle rebuff had bothered her.

As she meandered through the cemetery, tired but too awake yet to go back to the motel, she heard a grating sound nearby, stone dragging against stone. A dense clutch of shrubbery was on her left, and as she moved around it, a huge marble slab landed on the ground just feet away.

Beyond it, she saw an enormous demon, at least seven feet tall, dressed in what appeared to be ancient battle gear. A long battle-ax was strapped across his back. There was no question in her mind: This was Lagos.

"It's my lucky day," she said softly to herself.

With that, she ran at Lagos, leaped, and shot a hard side kick at his back. The demon barely flinched. He turned around and Faith slammed her fist into his face. Again, he seemed unfazed. She rained blow after blow down upon him.

Lagos only growled, picked her up by the throat, and threw her a dozen feet through the air to crash painfully into the side of a granite tomb. As if she was no trouble at all, Lagos returned to the smaller tomb he had opened and had been rummaging through when Faith had arrived. He reached within and retrieved something wrapped in old rags. Faith ran at him again, but Lagos slammed a huge fist into her gut and sent her flying backward. She landed painfully on her back, the wind knocked out of her.

Wheezing, trying to catch her breath, she rose slightly. Lagos picked up the rag-enshrouded package again, and stared at it. He bellowed with rage and threw the rags aside. Apparently, whatever he'd been looking for was not where he thought it would be.

Faith tried to rise, clutching her ribs, but the demon stomped off, ignoring her as if he had already forgotten she was there.

* * *

Across town, in Restfield Cemetery, Xander moved cautiously among the headstones and crypts. He was furious with himself, and very much hating his current situation.

"Hey, Giles," he said aloud, "here's an idea. Why don't I alleviate my guilt by going out and getting myself really, really killed?"

A moment later, he spotted the Von Hauptman family crypt. The door was open, and a scraping sound came from within. Heart racing wildly, Xander scurried for cover. A moment later, a dark figure emerged from the crypt, holding a bundle in its hands.

Xander stared in horror, suddenly unable to breathe.

It was Angel. The monster that had killed Jenny Calendar and nearly killed the rest of them, that had broken Buffy's heart. It was impossible. Buffy had killed him, sent him to Hell. But impossible or not, it was him.

After Angel was out of sight, Xander took three deep breaths to pull himself together, then set off after him. From inside his jacket, he pulled out a stake.

All the way across town to the mansion, he followed Angel. When he saw the vampire go inside, Xander slipped around the back to where stone stairs led down into the estate's garden. He was numb, still too astounded to believe it. In fear for his life, he cautiously crept across the garden to a dirty window at the back of the mansion, and peered inside.

Despite all that he had seen thus far, the sight that met his gaze now unnerved him more than anything else.

Angel. The monster. The killer.

Locked in a deep and passionate kiss with Buffy.

CHAPTER 3

In the back of Buffy's mind, a warning voice shrieked like an air-raid siren. She ignored it. Angel was in her arms, his lips were upon hers, his hands roamed over her body, and all was right with the world. Except it wasn't. As they pulled apart, eyes lingering upon the other's, she felt not the warm glow of her love for him, but horror at what it could lead to.

Angel without a soul. A merciless beast.

"Oh, God . . ." she whispered.

"Buffy—"

"What am I doing? What are *you* doing?"

He relented. "I don't know."

"Oh, God," she gasped, as she turned to walk away, to put some distance between them. "I don't even know why I came here."

Angel followed her, stopped her from leaving with a light touch on her arm. "It's good you did." He took her by the hand. "I think I have what you're looking for."

On a table sat an object wrapped in filthy rags.

"Great," Buffy said, staring at it. "Just, wherever this was gift-wrapped? Remind me not to shop there."

Angel unwrapped it to reveal a metal gauntlet, a dangerous-looking iron glove with spikes around the bottom where one's hand would slip inside.

"The Glove of Myhnegon," Angel explained.

"The world's ugliest fashion accessory." Buffy reached to touch it, but Angel stopped her. His hand felt electric over hers.

"Don't. Once you put it on, the glove can never be removed."

"So no touching," Buffy said, gaze resting on their intertwined fingers. "Kinda like us."

She took her hand away.

Angel covered up the glove again.

"You hold on to it," Buffy told him. "I'll tell Giles in the morning. At least he'll be happy."

Giles's eyes burned as he leafed through the pages of Volume III of *Tobin's Spirit Guide*. Mrs. Post paced across the apartment. It was very late, and it rankled in him even to have her in his home, but there was work to be done. He turned another page and felt a surge of exultation as he came upon an illustration.

"Ah. Yes, there we are. It's a wood engraving, see?"

Mrs. Post moved up beside his desk and looked over his shoulder.

"The Glove of Myhnegon," he announced proudly, reading the inscription beneath the image.

"Yes, engraved by Father Theodore of Wolsham, based, I believe, on very sketchy and unreliable folk legends. The pictures are fun to look at, Mr. Giles, but one really ought to read the nice words as well."

Her manner was insufferable as always. He had no idea how to respond, but was saved from having to do so when the kettle whistled on the stove in the narrow kitchen.

"Yes, well . . . some tea, perhaps," he murmured, then rose and went to the kitchen. He returned a moment later with a tray laden with cups and tea bags.

"I know you must find me tiresome," Mrs. Post admitted as she prepared her tea. "But it's insidious, really. A person slips up on the little things and soon everything's gone to hell in a handbasket. For example, Buffy, your Slayer—"

"Mrs. Post," Giles replied through gritted teeth, "I assure you Buffy is both dedicated and industrious. And I am in complete control of my Slayer."

As if on cue, Xander barreled into the apartment without so much as a knock. He looked pale and frightened, his clothes and hair in disarray.

"Giles," he said breathlessly. "We have a big problem. It's Buffy."

Mrs. Post raised an eyebrow. Giles ignored her.

"Will you excuse us?" he asked the other Watcher, silently damning Xander for his timing but far more concerned about what this horrible news might be.

Mrs. Post sipped at her tea. "Would you like some assistance?"

"Thank you, that won't be necessary."

Wednesday morning, before class, Buffy strolled into the library to report to Giles. "Lagos is outta luck. I found the magic mitten thingy!" she said happily.

The Slayer froze when she saw the grim faces on her friends. They were all there: Willow, Oz, Xander, Cordelia, and of course, Giles himself.

"What's with all the tragedy masks?"

None of them made any response at first. Then, a grave tone in his voice, Giles spoke up. "You'd better take a seat, Buffy."

Xander stood up and slid his chair over for her. The wind knocked out of her sails, Buffy slid into the chair at the study table, feeling all of their eyes upon her. "What's going on?"

"We know Angel is alive, Buffy. Xander saw you with him. It would appear that you've been hiding him and that you lied to us," Giles explained, voice tight with anger and pain.

"Nobody's here to blame you, Buffy," Willow added. "But this is serious. You need help."

Buffy could only stare at them for a moment as her mind searched for some explanation, some way to tell them. She hated the accusation she saw in their faces. They just did not understand what it had been like for her. How *could* they?

"It's . . . it's not what you think."

"I hope not," Xander said bluntly, no trace at all of humor in his voice. " 'Cause I think you're harboring a vicious killer."

"This isn't about attacking Buffy," Willow chided him. "Remember, 'I' statements only. 'I feel angry.' 'I feel worried.' "

"Fine," Cordelia said snippily. "Here's one. I feel worried—about me! Last time around, Angel barely laid a hand on Buffy. He was way more interested in killing her friends."

"But he's better now," Buffy argued, wishing she could make them understand.

"Better for how long, Buffy? I mean, did you even think about that?" Xander countered.

The Slayer stood up, angry at them. "What is this, Demons Anonymous? I don't need an intervention here."

She began to walk away, but Giles's voice stopped her.

"Oh, don't you?" he asked. "You must have known it was wrong seeing him or you wouldn't have hidden it from all of us."

"I was going to tell you. I was," she protested, her voice thick with emotion. "It was just that I didn't know why he came back. I just wanted to wait—"

"For what?" Xander snapped bitterly. "For Angel to go psycho again the next time you give him a happy?"

"I'm not going to!" Buffy retorted angrily. "We're not together like that."

Oz had sat through all of it in silence, as usual. Now, from the corner, he spoke up. "But you *were* kissing him."

Buffy blinked, stunned by what those words meant. She could not deny the truth in them, but anger boiled in her as she realized how that truth had most likely been discovered. She turned to Xander.

"You were spying on me? What gives you the right?"

Cordelia wasn't having it. "What gives *you* the right to suck face with your demon lover again?"

"It was an accident!"

Xander stared at her. "What, you just tripped and fell on his lips?"

"It was wrong, okay? I know that and I know that it can't happen again. But you guys have to believe me, I would never put you in any danger. If I thought for a second that Angel was going to hurt anyone—"

"You would stop him," Xander cut in, voice tinged with sarcasm. "Like you did last time, with Miss Calendar."

Buffy stared at him, horrified to think that he might actually blame her for Jenny Calendar's death. She had no response. Could not have ever imagined needing one.

Willow spoke up quietly. "Buffy . . . I feel, that when it comes to Angel? You can't see straight. And that's why we're all gonna help you face this."

"But he's better now, I swear. Look, you guys, he's the one who found the Glove of Myhnegon. He's keeping it safe for us in the mansion."

"Right!" Xander shouted. "Good plan. Leave tons of

firepower with the scary guy. And leave us to clean up the mess."

Furious, he stormed toward the door.

Buffy grabbed his arm and he spun to face her. "You would just love an excuse to hurt him, wouldn't you?"

"I don't need an excuse," Xander replied darkly. "I think lots of dead people actually constitutes a reason."

"Right. This is all nobility. This has nothing to do with jealousy," Buffy said, certain the the crush he'd once had on her was at least part of his motivation for being so angry.

"Hello?" Cordelia chimed in. "Miss Not-Over-Yourself-Yet?"

"Don't you start with me," Buffy snapped.

Panicked, Willow turned to the Watcher. "Giles, no one's doing the 'I' statements."

"That's enough!" Giles said curtly. "Everybody. Buffy knows our concerns. Her actions, however ill-advised, can be understood. Our priority right now is to retrieve the Glove of Myhnegon and try to destroy it. Now all of you back to class."

Without another word, they all rose and filed out of the library. Buffy watched them go, a deep sadness filling her. But at least Giles had stood up for her. He went into his inner office and after the others had gone, she followed him in. His back was to her.

"Thanks . . . for the bail in there," she said tentatively. "I know this is a lot to absorb, but Angel did find the glove, and there was a—"

"Be quiet."

Two simple words that froze her completely. Still, Giles did not look at her. Buffy had heard the pain in his voice, and she could not bear it that he would not meet her eyes. Finally, he began to turn.

"I won't remind you that the fate of the world often rests with the Slayer. What would be the point? Nor shall I re-

mind you that you've jeopardized the lives of all whom
you hold dear, by harboring a known murderer. But sadly I
must remind you that Angel *tortured* me. For hours. For
pleasure. You should have told me he was alive. You didn't.
You have no respect for me, or the job I perform."

With that he turned and sat at his desk, freezing her
out. After a moment, Buffy turned to go.

She had never felt so alone.

In the drab motel room where she had been staying since
her arrival in Sunnydale, Faith stared numbly at the television screen. After Buffy had snubbed her when she tried to
get some girl talk going between them, she had retreated
back to the patterns of her first couple of weeks in town.
Whenever she wasn't on call as a Slayer, she lingered in the
room, shadow-boxing or working out or watching something on television that would kill a few more brain cells.

Bored, she got up and clicked off the tube.

There was a knock at the door.

Faith wasn't expecting anyone. She grabbed a stake,
pulled the door open, and nearly drove that sharpened
wooden shaft into the chest of her Watcher, Mrs. Post.
She lowered the stake, though a little voice in the back of
her head pointed out that it might have been better if
she'd just staked away.

"A word of advice," Mrs. Post said, an uncharacteristic
smile on her face. "Vampires rarely knock. Especially in
daylight."

Faith didn't bother to mention that the last unexpected
visitor she'd had was the vampire Kakistos. He had
knocked, and then he'd nearly killed both her and Buffy.
But she figured Mrs. Post would not take kindly to being
corrected.

"So . . . this is your home?" the Watcher asked, glancing around with obvious distaste.

"Yeah," Faith replied, not bothering to hide the sarcasm. "The decorator actually just left."

"Faith, do you know who the Spartans were?" Mrs. Post inquired.

"Wild stab," Faith replied, dropping onto the bed. "A bunch of guys from Spart?"

Mrs. Post leaned against the bureau. "They were the fiercest warriors known to ancient Greece. And they lived in quarters very much like these. Do you know why?"

Faith shrugged, but she was listening.

"Because a true fighter needs nothing else. I'm going to be very hard on you, Faith. I will not brook insolence or laziness. And I will not allow blunders like last night's attack. You will probably hate me a great deal of the time."

"Ya think?" she teased.

But even as she spoke, she had begun to think that maybe she had not given Mrs. Post enough of a chance. She liked all the warrior talk. Mrs. Post was a little light on the social skills, but she had an edge and a determination that Faith felt in herself. Like Giles, the woman did seem to really want what was best for her. It wasn't easy for her to trust. She'd trusted Buffy, before the other Slayer had started to push her away. Now she had to decide if she trusted Mrs. Post, too.

"I will make you a better Slayer," the woman went on, "and that will keep you alive. You have to trust that I'm right. God only knows what Mr. Giles has been filling your head with."

"Giles is okay," Faith argued.

"His methods are unfathomable to me," Mrs. Post replied. "I find him entirely confounding. But that is not important. Let him have his games and secret meetings."

"What meetings?" Faith asked.

"I don't know. Something with Buffy and her friends."

"Oh," Faith muttered. "I guess that doesn't include me."

Buffy and her friends. The words hurt. Her first Watcher had given her reason to feel like part of something greater. Faith had never felt that way before. Then the woman had been murdered and she had been unable to prevent it. Upon her arrival in Sunnydale, Faith had promised herself time and time again that she would not allow herself to hope for such a thing again, for that sense of belonging, of home. And yet the feeling had begun to grow in her anyway. *Buffy and her friends.* But where did Faith fit in all that? The horrible suspicion that filled her was that she didn't fit in at all. There was only ever supposed to be one Slayer. She was extra, expendable . . . what was the word? Redundant.

For the past few weeks, Faith and Buffy had been getting closer, but after the way the other Slayer had shut her out the night before, and now this . . .

"And why does he let her socialize that much?" Mrs. Post went on. "It hardly seems . . . no matter. Would you like to do some training?"

Yeah, all that socialization, Faith thought bitterly. Her own social life was pretty much the grimy motel room they were standing in. Lips pressed together in a tight line, she studied Mrs. Post.

"Training, as in kicking, punching, stabbing?" It sounded good to her.

"That's the idea."

"I'm your girl."

The bell sounded, signaling the end to another school day. It was the nicest sound in the world. Buffy watched Willow walk to her locker and stuff a huge number of books inside. After a moment, she took a deep breath and walked over.

"Hey," she said, tentatively.

"Hey!" Willow replied amiably.

"So on a scale of one to a million, how much are you hating me right now?"

"Zero," Willow assured her. "You were scared. You kept a secret, y'know? It's okay. Secrets aren't bad, y'know, they're normal. They're better than normal, they're good. Secrets are good. Must be a reason why we keep 'em, right?"

"I guess," Buffy replied, a bit confused by Willow's enthusiastic response.

They walked down the corridor together.

"So, you going to the Bronze tonight, or are you gonna sneak away for a not-so-secret rendezvous with Angel?" Willow pried.

"None of the above. I'm gonna try and kill this Lagos guy. Peace offering to Giles."

"Well, Angel has the glove now, right?"

"Yep. But Lagos doesn't know that. I figure sooner or later he's bound to show up at that crypt looking for it," Buffy reasoned.

"Ah, but instead he finds a Buffy in a not so good mood."

"That's my brilliant plan."

When Faith strolled into the Bronze, the last thing she expected to see was Xander Harris playing pool by himself. She had been hesitant to hit the club because she really did not want to see Buffy at the moment unless she had to. Though she would barely admit it to herself, she was smarting from the way she felt she had been excluded, even cast aside, the last few days. All she wanted from the Bronze was to burn off a little energy, find a few willing dance partners and get them all feverish. With guys like that, she could see herself from their perspective for a little while, as magnificent and dark and sexy as they thought she was.

But now here was Xander.

From the moment they had met, she had thought he was a little goofy, but cute. He looked better than cute just now, in a button-down shirt that hung on him just so, with a gray tee beneath. He looked a bit messy, and more than a little angry, like he was blowing off steam.

Join the club, Faith thought.

He racked the balls up again, then lined up his cue and broke, multicolored balls scattering all over the table.

"You look pissed," Faith told him.

He glanced up at her, then back at the table. "Rough day."

"Tell me about it."

"I'd rather just shoot," he replied.

Faith frowned. Whatever his beef was, boys did not dismiss her like that. Not ever. She thought about the meeting Buffy and her friends were supposed to have had, and it gave her fresh anger to work from.

"Don't think I don't know what you and your pals were talking about behind my back today." Faith leaned on the table.

"Yeah? And what was that?"

She pressed him. They didn't want her to be a part of what they were doing, but they couldn't stop her, either. Buffy wasn't the only Slayer in town. "More about this glove deal than you're saying," she replied.

"The Glove of Myhnegon?" he scoffed. "Right. How'd you like a hit of some real news? Angel's still alive."

Xander shot another ball.

Faith raised her eyebrows. "The vampire."

"Back in town. Saw him myself. Toting the popular and famous glove."

"Angel," Faith mused, pleased with the thought of having someone to slay. "Guy like that, with that kind of glove, could kill a whole mess of people."

"Said the same thing to Buffy myself," Xander muttered. "Weird how she didn't seem to care."

Faith gaped at him. "Buffy knew he was alive? I can't believe her!"

She thought of all the times Buffy had seemed distracted recently, all the things she had revealed about herself, the questions she had asked Buffy, trying to know her better. It was like a cruel joke, the idea that all that time Buffy had been hiding this, and the joke was on Faith. Anger roiled up inside her, swelling into rage.

She liked the feeling.

"She says he's clean," Xander explained, though it was clear from his tone that he didn't believe it.

"Yeah, well, I say we can't afford to find out," Faith replied, in the groove. "I say I deal with this problem right now. I say I slay."

Xander cracked off one last shot on the pool table, then stood and fixed her with a steady, grim look. "Can I come?"

Giles sat in his office nervously arranging his books before him. He had prepared a small presentation for Mrs. Post. He heard her footsteps out in the library and turned as she entered.

"You wanted to see me, Mr. Giles?"

"Yes. I do apologize for bringing you in at this late hour," he began.

"Please. A good Watcher must be awake and alert at all hours."

Despite her words, Giles sensed that Mrs. Post was more tired than she wanted to reveal. She looked less severe to him tonight, her hair down and without her glasses.

"Would you like some tea?" he asked.

"God, yes, please," she sighed. "I'm completely knackered."

She walked slowly to his desk chair as Giles went to a

sideboard to prepare the tea. Mrs. Post slid into the chair.

"I spent the afternoon training with Faith," Mrs. Post revealed. "She doesn't lack for energy."

Giles chuckled good-naturedly. "She's your first Slayer, I take it?"

"If you're questioning my qualifications—"

"I'm not. I have complete respect for your methods in my own, American way."

She smiled a bit.

"I also have the glove. It's not actually on me, but I believe it's safe. It's in a mansion on Crawford Street. A . . . friend of Buffy's keeping it there."

"We must get to it," she said quickly. "Immediately. Hide it, before someone else finds it."

"Or better still, destroy it," Giles suggested.

"Destroy it?"

Giles picked up a lavishly illustrated Latin text and presented it to her. "Yes, I didn't think it could be done, either. It requires transforming fire into Living Flame and immolating the glove. It's complex, but I believe I have all the necessary materials."

He placed the book back on the desk and flipped a few pages.

"Well, I must say, Mr. Giles, good show," Mrs. Post said.

Giles was quite pleased with the compliment. Right up until the moment she cracked him on the head with a Malaysian fertility idol she'd picked up from a shelf.

Pain rocketed into his brain and he slumped over the desk. Struggling to stay upright, he turned to look at her.

"Good show indeed," she whispered, a broad smile on her face.

Then she struck him again, and Giles slid to the floor as the world dimmed around him. He felt as though he were falling into a deep well, and then there was only darkness.

CHAPTER 4

The wind that swept across Restfield Cemetery that night seemed colder than usual. Willow shivered as she paced in front of the Von Hauptman family crypt. Buffy sat on a stone bench across from the tomb, impassive. Willow wished she could be that calm, but she had a lot on her mind. Aside from the guilt from her kiss with Xander, a secret that felt as though it was burning its way through her, there was the whole not-wanting-to-die thing.

They were waiting for Lagos to come back for the glove.

Willow could think of a great many things she would rather be doing.

"Um, not to downplay my own slaying abilities, which in some circles are considered formidable," she ventured, "but, shouldn't Faith be here?"

"I tried calling but nobody was home. But if you're feeling any demon-o-phobia, please . . . splitting is totally an option. You're not the one in trouble with Giles."

"That's true," Willow said tentatively, though her mind

went back to the kiss, the library, and her fear that Giles had seen her and Xander.

Buffy did not notice her hesitation. "How long do you think he can stay mad at me, anyway?"

"The emotional Marathon Man?" Willow shrugged.

"I can't really blame him," Buffy admitted. "It's weird, though. Now that my secret . . . Angel . . . it's all out in the open, I feel better."

"Well, sure you do," Willow replied emphatically. "This big burden's been lifted. I mean, keeping secrets is a lot of work . . . one could hypothetically imagine."

"You have no idea."

Willow flushed a bit. "None whatsoever. But . . ." she sat down next to Buffy on the bench. "Can I ask you a question? When you were with Angel and nobody knew about it, did that make it feel, y'know, sexier somehow?"

"Not really. It's too much pressure. After a while it even makes the fun parts not so fun."

"Huh."

"What makes you think all this secret stuff is sexy, anyway?"

"Nothing," Willow said quickly, panic flooding her. "I'm just wondering. Gotta keep asking the big old questions when you're blessed with this girl's thirst for knowledge and . . . okay. There's something I have to tell you."

Buffy watched her curiously. "What?"

Willow stood up and started pacing again. "Okay, this'll make me feel better, right? Y'know, I've always thought of myself as a good person. Floss, do my homework, never cheat. But lately, and please don't judge me on this, but . . . I want you to be the first to know that—"

Something moved in the dark beyond Buffy. Willow's eyes went wide.

"There's a demon behind you."

Buffy sprang from the bench and turned. Both girls

were startled by the ugly warrior demon striding toward them. From Faith's description, they knew it was Lagos.

In a single, fluid motion, Buffy ran at the demon and leaped up to drop-kick it with both feet, right in the center of the chest. It barely noticed. She landed and was up again in an instant, but Lagos lifted her into his huge hands and slammed her to the ground. Fast as she was able, Buffy rose and started to pummel him. The demon's head snapped back and she rained blows down upon him.

Lagos picked her up as though she were a rag doll, hefted her above his head, and threw her to the ground again. She barely moved out of his way in time to avoid a killing blow, but then she was up once more. Buffy dodged and Lagos's huge fist shattered a gravestone to powder. The Slayer moved in, struck him with several thunderous blows, then kicked him in the gut. The demon doubled over, and Buffy spotted the huge battle-ax that was slung across his back.

"Now we're talking," she muttered as she tore the ax away from him.

With a single swipe, she decapitated the demon. His enormous head thunked to the ground, bounced once, then rolled to a stop.

Willow gave her a thumbs up. "Yes!"

Buffy walked back to her, ax in hand. "Sorry about that. So, what were you going to tell me?"

"Oh, I . . ." Willow began. But she had lost her nerve. "I opened my S.A.T. test booklet five minutes early. Just doesn't seem important now, does it?"

Buffy smiled. "Your secret's safe with me." She slung the ax over her shoulder. "Come on. Let's go bring Giles some happiness."

As Faith stormed down the corridor late that night with Xander at her side, her only point of anxiety was whether or not there would be anyone in the library. Not that she could think of a single reason why anyone except Buffy would want to stop them from dusting Angel. Willow might have mixed feelings about it, but even she could not argue that it was the safest course of action.

The library doors slammed open as they pushed through.

"Good old Sunnydale library. Fully equipped with reference books, file cards . . ." Xander strode across to an ominously large metal cabinet on the far wall and flung the doors open, ". . . and weapons."

The cabinet was filled with swords, maces, axes, throwing stars, and other implements of war.

"Beauty," Faith said.

Xander reached into the cabinet. "I call crossbow."

"You got it."

They loaded up on weapons and Xander slammed the cabinet shut.

"All right, ready to go?"

"That I am," Faith replied.

As they turned and headed for the doors, however, Xander heard a groan. He glanced around, and heard it again.

"Wait," he said.

"What?"

It came again, louder, and this time they pinpointed its source. It was coming from the inner office. Swiftly, Xander went through the door. Inside, the Watcher lay unconscious on the floor, limbs akimbo, a sticky patch of blood in his hair.

"Oh, my God, it's Giles." He knelt by the Watcher. "Giles, can you hear me?" Xander looked around the office. "What the hell happened?"

"Gee," Faith drawled cynically from the doorway, "let me guess."

"Stop," he told her. "Hold it, just think a minute."

"Yeah, I'm *thinking*," she snapped. "Thinking Buffy's ex-meat did this."

Xander grabbed the phone off Giles's desk, and turned to her as he lifted it off the cradle. "It's not Angel's style." He dialed 911.

"The guy's a demon. How much more proof do you need?" Faith sneered at him.

"Bite marks would be nice," he retorted, even as he heard someone pick up on the other end of the line. "Yeah, I have a medical emergency. Sunnydale High."

Faith spun away from him. "Screw this waiting crap," she muttered as she stormed out.

Angrily, Xander shouted after her. "Faith, if we leave, Giles could die!"

"Yeah, and he's gonna have a whole lot of company unless I do something permanent." She didn't even slow down.

"Wait!"

Furious, she stopped near the door and turned around. "For what? You to grow a pair? You handle the baby-sit and I'm gonna kill Angel."

Clearly Xander was tempted to go after her, but one look at the blood on Giles's scalp and Faith knew he would stay. She stalked out, leaving him by the Watcher, hearing him mutter.

"Dammit."

Though she had been burdened with profound guilt before, Buffy felt better now that she had killed Lagos. It would not make up for her failing to tell Giles of Angel's return, but it would please him, at least. That was something.

"Giles has to be psyched that we showed up stuffy old Mrs. Post," she said, as she and Willow entered the library together.

Then she glanced away from her friend's smile and froze at the sight that unfolded before her.

"Oh, my God," Buffy whispered.

A team of paramedics surrounded Giles, who lay quite still on a stretcher, while Xander looked on. One of them checked the Watcher's pulse while another bandaged his head. There was blood on the bandages. Buffy felt her heart race with her fear for him. She tossed Lagos's battle-ax over the checkout counter and ran toward him.

"What happened?" she demanded.

The lead paramedic was on the two-way radio clipped to her belt. "Sunnydale Medical, we have a Caucasian male, mid-forties, blunt object head trauma. Notify E.R. we're bringing him in."

"What happened?" Buffy snapped at her.

"No time for this," the paramedic replied.

"Wait," Giles called weakly. "Buffy . . . you must . . . destroy the glove."

"You want him to live?" the lead paramedic asked callously. "Get out of the way."

As they hustled the gurney out of the library, Giles raised a shaky hand. "Use . . . Living Flame," he rasped.

Then they were gone, and the Watcher with them. Frantic, Buffy stared at Xander, and asked the question for the third time.

"What happened?"

"Your boyfriend's not as cured as you thought," Xander said bluntly.

Buffy shook her head. "What makes you think that Angel had anything to do with this?"

"We saw what you saw."

"So you just assume?" Buffy snapped.

"I didn't," Xander replied. "Faith did."

Cold fingers gripped Buffy's heart as dread spread through her. "What did you tell her?"

"Only what everyone knows. She's a big girl. Came to her own conclusions."

Angry now, Buffy glared at him. "How much of a head start does she have?"

He shrugged. "Ten minutes."

Pulse racing, she turned to Willow. "Go through Giles's research. Figure out how to destroy the glove." Buffy cast a last glance of horror and disbelief at Xander, then she ran for the doors.

Just before she reached them, she heard Willow snap at Xander.

"Shut up and help me!"

Buffy knew Willow would come through for her. She only hoped she reached Angel in time.

Angel stood alone in the main chamber of the mansion. In a large brazier upon an iron stand before him, flames rose and flickered. From a small table beside it—laden with herbs and many magickal ingredients—he picked a handful of grainy powder up in his hand and sifted a bit from his fingers before sprinkling it over the blaze. The flames reached eerie tendrils up, raging for a moment, before withdrawing again.

"*Exorere, Flamma Vitae,*" he intoned, the Latin coming easily to his lips, though he had rarely spoken it these last hundred years. "*Prodi ex loco tuo elementorum, in hunc mundum vivorum.*"

He picked up a different jar of powder, poured a bit into his hand and tossed it into the flames. They surged up again, and the edges of the flickering fire turned green.

Once more, Angel intoned the spell, even as he lifted a third jar. This time, when he sprinkled the fire, it blazed up with a life all its own, raging brightly like a being unto itself. Which it was. This was Living Flame. Its eerie light danced across the gray stone walls.

He sensed motion behind him, and turned, on guard, to

see a primly dressed, vaguely attractive human woman enter the room.

"What do you want?"

"Gwen Post," the woman replied. "Mr. Giles sent me." Angel frowned, studying her. "What for?"

"To help you destroy the glove. Is that the Living Flame?"

"Yes," he allowed, keeping his gaze locked on her. He did not trust this newcomer. Not at all.

The woman paused to regard him, perhaps sensing his hesitation. "Look, I'm sorry to be abrupt, but Lagos is on his way here now. If you're performing the ritual incorrectly, it will only make the glove more powerful."

"All right," he relented. The ritual had exhausted what little strength he had these days. It might have been that he was on edge because of that. As long as he kept an eye on the Post woman, he thought he might as well go along with her. He could not chance the question of whether or not to trust her.

"Good. Where is the glove?"

"It's in the trunk," he told her, gesturing toward a huge, antique traveling case on the other side of the room by the fireplace.

He turned to get it. Angel heard the scrape of metal on metal as she picked up the shovel he had used to dig up Cadlin root for the ritual, but he turned too slowly.

The shovel connected solidly with the back of his head and he went down hard.

"That's what I love about this town," she said, even as he started to black out. "Everyone is so helpful."

As if he were already dead, Mrs. Post crossed the room to the trunk, only to find it padlocked. She swore under her breath, then hefted the shovel again and shattered the lock.

Angel stood up behind her. His face had changed, the

forehead now ridged and demonic, fangs lengthening, eyes blazing inhumanly.

"Okay, that hurt," he informed her, danger in his now-guttural voice.

Startled, Mrs. Post turned and flinched in surprise when she realized that he was a vampire. But she recovered quickly enough.

"It was supposed to kill you," she said, almost kindly. "If you'd been human, it would have. But . . ." she cracked the shovel over her knee and dropped the metal end, leaving only a length of splintered wood in her hand. An instant stake. "I believe this is your poison."

Mrs. Post lunged at him with the wooden shaft. He ducked her first attack, blocked the second, and then hammered her to the ground. In a rage, he rushed at her as she rose, and then slammed Mrs. Post against the stone wall. She struck her head and crumbled to the ground, unconscious.

Just at the very moment that Faith burst in the door.

"Mrs. Post!" she cried, seeing Angel in full vamp-face and her Watcher lying unconscious on the floor.

She glared at him, eyes filled with hate. "I can't believe how much I'm gonna enjoy killing you."

CHAPTER 5

In the library, Willow and Xander mixed a horrible-smelling concoction in a glass bowl, using Giles's mortar and pestle. She had gone through all of his notes, and believed they had done everything correctly. But Willow could read Latin only passably, and Xander could sound out the words but had no idea what they meant.

"Think we got it?" Xander asked doubtfully.

"Well, it's either the catalyst for Living Flame, or just some really smelly sand. We'll have to test this," she said with regret, knowing that time was short.

"I'll double-check." He glanced at Giles's notes again. Willow saw his eyes light up. And not in a good way.

"What?" she asked, concerned.

"I know what the glove does," he said grimly, then he showed her the page.

Her heart sank. "There's no time to test this," Willow said.

She held up a small plastic bag and Xander poured the

mixture into it. Together, they ran from the library, knowing that the clock was ticking.

Faith stared at Angel in horror. This monster, this demon, had attacked Giles and then Mrs. Post. As far as she knew, Giles was still alive, but she couldn't tell if her own Watcher was even breathing. In her brief time as Slayer, she had seen one Watcher slaughtered by a vampire before her eyes. No way was she going to let it happen again.

"You're not getting that glove," Angel snarled, fangs glistening in the light from the magickal flame that danced on a brazier nearby.

"Wanna bet?" Faith snapped.

She would get the glove. A monster as deadly as Angel? No way was she going to leave it in his hands. Faith gripped the gaffing hook she had pulled from Giles's weapons cabinet and rushed him.

Angel batted the hook from her hand. Faith slammed into his chest, and he struck her with a solid backhand that rocked her head back. Fury redoubled within her. Her fist connected with his face, but when he swung to repay the favor, she dodged to one side and brought her leg up backward to deliver a hard kick to the head.

While he reeled, she stomped on the back of his leg, driving him down. Using all her strength, she tossed him over the couch, where he slammed into the coffee table. He lay there for a moment, trying to get his bearings. Faith didn't give him a chance.

Running around the couch, she withdrew a stake from inside her jacket. With both hands, she raised it over her head and brought it down.

From out of nowhere, Buffy appeared. She grabbed Faith by the wrists, stopping her before she could dust Angel.

"What?" Faith muttered.

Buffy threw her backward. Faith recovered in an instant, and the two Slayers faced off against each other. Though she had once thought they could be friends, Faith realized that she had always known it might come to this. But she had never imagined it would be her trying to stop Buffy from doing something awful, rather than the other way around.

"I can't let you do it, Faith," Buffy said, regret in her voice.

Faith smiled, but there was nothing friendly in it. "You're confused, Twinkie. Let me clear you up." She pointed at Angel with the stake. "Vampire." Then at herself. "Slayer." Back at Angel. "Dead vampire."

"There's a lot that you don't understand."

A voice called weakly from across the room. "Faith . . ."

They both glanced over.

Mrs. Post had regained consciousness, much the worse for wear, and struggled to rise. "She doesn't know. She's blinded by love."

"Faith, no," Buffy said, emphatically.

"Trust me," Mrs. Post rasped.

Buffy shook her head. "Faith, we can figure this out."

But Faith had already figured it out, as much as she cared to. Buffy had betrayed her. Mrs. Post had earned her trust. And Angel . . . he was a vampire.

With a spinning kick, Faith drove Buffy to the ground. But Buffy didn't stay down. She was up in an eyeblink—less—and the blow she hammered at Faith rocked her backward. Faith hit Buffy again, but with each of her blows, Buffy got in three. The two girls battered at one another, and then Faith went down hard.

Again she was up, facing off against Buffy. They were too evenly matched. They spun and kicked, and most of their blows connected. Faith was groggy, but she ducked a kick, then slammed Buffy with one of her own. The other Slayer grunted and went down, but Faith was right behind her. She wrapped an arm around Buffy's throat and began to choke her.

Buffy grappled for her hands, trying to free herself. She snagged one of Faith's fingers and pulled, hard enough that something cracked. Faith cried out in pain and Buffy tossed her off into a stone corner that jammed into her back. As Buffy ran at her, Faith swept a leg around and knocked her off her feet.

Once more, she was up. As Buffy rose, Faith launched a high kick at her face, but the other Slayer caught her foot in the air and shoved her backward toward a pair of French doors. As Faith recovered, Buffy hurtled at her across the room and together they crashed through the glass doors, shards flying all around them.

Outside, on a patio in the dead garden, the fight continued.

Xander was the first to rush in the front door, but Willow was right behind him. When they saw Mrs. Post, bruised and rumpled, Willow gasped. They ran to her.

"The glove," she said, wincing with pain, "it's in the trunk."

"We'll get it," Xander vowed.

Mrs. Post nodded gratefully. "Help Faith," she pleaded.

With a glance out through the shattered doors, he saw the two Slayers pummeling each other on the patio. Xander cursed under his breath as he raced out to intervene.

"What are you . . . stop!" he snapped. "Guys, listen!"

Xander stepped between them and Faith backhanded him, hard. With a grunt, Xander tumbled into a corner of the patio. When he looked up, he saw Buffy jump and come down with her fist, driving Faith to her knees.

Willow watched as Mrs. Post hurried to the trunk and flung open the top. It seemed odd to her that the woman was suddenly so energetic, but she figured it was just the intensity of the situation.

Mrs. Post reached into the trunk, threw back some dirty rags, and lifted out the glove.

"Finally," she said.

Then she turned and cracked Willow in the side of the head with the heavy metal artifact. Willow fell hard, then looked up through a haze of pain as Mrs. Post slipped her hand into the glove. Thick metal prongs like spider's legs made a circle around the bottom of it, and when the woman put it on, the prongs snapped closed one by one, sinking into the flesh of Mrs. Post's forearm.

Willow winced as if the pain had been her own, but she was amazed to see that the Watcher seemed impervious to the pain. Mrs. Post raised the glove toward the enormous skylight, through which the stars were visible.

"*Tar chugam a chumhacht Myhnegon!*" Mrs. Post screamed.

Thunder rolled across the sky. Willow struggled to understand the words—which she thought were Gaelic—then realized it didn't matter. The woman's intentions were clear enough.

With a grunt, Buffy cracked her knuckles across Faith's face in a savage backhand. Faith struck back, but Buffy trapped her fist. At the boom of the thunder, both Slayers froze and stared up at the sky. As one, they peered through the shattered French doors and into Angel's home, where Mrs. Post stood, arm raised high, the Glove of Myhnegon almost glowing with preternatural light on her hand.

"What's going on?" Faith asked. But even as she said the words, she realized: she had been deceived. They all had.

With a wide grin, Mrs. Post turned to look at them. "Faith, a word of advice. You're an idiot." She thrust the glove toward the sky again, and cried out. "*Tar frim!*"

Sorcerous energy shot down from the sky like a bolt of lightning, shattering the skylight and surging through the glove. It crackled with power as glass shards poured down.

Mrs. Post turned toward the Slayers and pointed with the glove. Tendrils of crackling energy lanced out at them. Buffy tackled Faith out of the way, and the lightning struck a tree outside, causing it to burst into flames.

Inside the room, Angel, groggy, began to rise. He saw Willow. Alone in the middle of the room. Nothing to protect her.

Mrs. Post turned and shouted the enchantment again. Willow was a sitting duck. Buffy and Faith were much too far away to help, but they need not have worried. Even as the surge of mystical power sparked out toward her friend, Angel lunged across the room and knocked Willow out of the way.

Grim, but determined, Buffy turned to Faith. Faith understood: whatever had happened between them, they had to be together now.

"Can you draw her fire?" she asked.

"You bet I can," Faith replied coldly.

"Go to it."

As Faith got up and went for Mrs. Post, Buffy glanced desperately around, searching for the largest piece of broken glass she could find. Inside the house, she heard Mrs. Post shout again, and the explosion as another bolt of supernatural lightning crackled across the room. She saw Faith streaking around the chamber, distracting Mrs. Post from the patio and Willow and Angel.

Buffy picked up a huge piece of glass from the patio floor, large enough that it was practically a complete pane from the broken French doors.

"There's nothing you can do to me now!" Mrs. Post

called to Faith within. "I have the glove. With the glove comes the power."

Buffy stepped through the shattered doors. "I'm getting that," she said.

Once more Mrs. Post cried out for the power to come into her. In that same instant, Buffy hurled the razor-sharp glass like a discus. It spun through the air and sliced Mrs. Post's arm off, just above the elbow. Still inside the glove, her arm clanked to the floor.

But the circuit of dark power still existed. The woman had called upon the power, and another bolt of mystical energy struck like lightning from above. Without the glove on, it fried Mrs. Post where she stood. Tendrils of the energy crackled around her as she shrieked in agony. Her skin burned, then blackened, but the lightning continued, until she imploded in a flash of power, leaving nothing behind but the glove, and a dead woman's arm.

All around the room, they began to rise. Willow, Angel, and Faith. Xander stumbled in from the patio. Slowly, they walked toward the center of the room where the smoke still rose from the woman's horrible death. They stared at the arm.

When the spider-prongs suddenly retracted one by one from the dead flesh, they all jumped, just a little.

The following morning, Willow sat in the student lounge with Oz, his arm slung casually over her shoulder. Xander and Cordelia were across from them. It was much needed down time.

"So there's no more glove thingy?" Cordelia asked hopefully.

"A little Living Flame, a little mesquite . . . gone for good," Xander reassured her.

Oz nodded once. "Sounds like we missed a lot of fun."

"Then we're telling it wrong," Xander countered.

"What do you think Buffy and Angel are gonna do?" Willow asked.

Xander offered a tiny shrug. "Boy, do I don't know."

"Well," Willow said slowly, "he saved me from a horrible, flamey death. That sorta makes me like him again."

"As long as she and Angel don't get pelvic, we'll be okay, I guess," Xander observed.

A moment later, Buffy walked over, beautiful in black and beige. But that beauty stopped at her eyes, which were filled with anxiety. She seemed to hesitate for a moment before speaking.

"What are you guys talking about?"

"Oddly enough, your boyfriend. Again," Oz informed her.

With a forlorn sigh, she sat. "He's not my boyfriend. Really and truly. He's . . . I don't know." She turned cautiously to Xander. "Are we cool?"

"Yeah," he said, a little too lightly. Then his voice lowered and he became more serious. "Just . . . seeing the two of you kissing, after everything that happened . . . I leaned toward the postal. But I trust you."

"I don't," Cordelia sniped. "Just for the record."

A few feet away, Giles cleared his voice. They all turned toward him. He held a cup of tea in one hand, and was a bit pitiful with the bandage on his head.

"Let me guess," Buffy ventured. "Gwendolyn Post, not a Watcher?"

"Yes, she was," he revealed. "She was kicked out of the Council a couple of years ago for misuses of dark power. They swear there was a memo."

Buffy nodded. "Well, I'd better go. Little more damage control."

After she had gone off, Willow sighed deeply.

"The whole Angel thing is so weird."

Faith

"I'm going to go out on a limb and say we've got a new Slayer in town."

Kakistos

Angel is back.

Gwendolyn Post

Faith's livin' large. . . .

Consequences

Giles sat slowly in the seat Buffy had vacated. "Yes, well, we'll have to see how that unfolds, won't we?"

Faith sat in her run-down motel room and watched a lot of nothing on TV while flipping through a magazine.

The knock at the door surprised her.

"Come in," she called.

Buffy opened the door and stepped inside. "Hey."

Faith would not look at her. Too many things whirled in her head, the things she had allowed herself to hope, and the way she had felt when she discovered that she had been deceived. Of course, Buffy had hidden her secret from everyone, but even when it had come out, Faith doubted the idea of telling *her* the truth had ever even come up.

"Place looks nice," Buffy noted.

"Yeah, it's real Spartan," Faith replied coldly.

There was a pause before Buffy continued.

"How are you?"

"Five by five."

"I'll interpret that as good." Buffy sighed. "Look, Gwendolyn Post, or whoever she may be, had us all fooled. Even Giles."

"Yeah, well, you can't trust people. I should've learned that by now," Faith observed bitterly. She was certain Buffy would get the point.

Deep down Faith understood, at least a little, why Buffy had done what she had done. And she had not forgotten the way she had felt in the times when it was just the two of them. As Slayers, they were a breed of two. *That ought to mean something,* Faith thought.

She just could not be sure if it really did.

"I realize this is gonna sound funny coming from someone who just spent a lot of time kicking your face, but you can trust *me*," Buffy told her.

Faith finally looked at her, not amused. "Is that right?"

"I know I've kept secrets. But I didn't have a choice. I'm on your side."

"I'm on my side," Faith retorted coldly. "And that's enough."

"Not always," Buffy argued.

Yeah, always, Faith thought. *That's the way it has to be.*

"Is that it?" she asked.

With a hurt expression, Buffy nodded. "Yeah, I guess."

"All right. Well, then, I'll see you," Faith said, dismissing her.

Buffy turned to go. Faith looked down, doubt and hurt and hope all battling inside her. "Buffy?" she ventured.

"Yeah?" Buffy said.

But when the Slayer turned to face her, Faith pushed it all away. She had let too many people in lately, and had nothing but pain in return.

Faith almost spoke up. Instead she just shook her head. "Nothing."

Buffy left, and Faith was alone.

Again.

Outside the Schoolyard

So much has changed . . .

Faith was walking again. She had taken, lately, to exploring the areas of Sunnydale that weren't all bright and shiny. Despite what the average tourist would think, cruising through downtown and checking out the college and the beach, there were plenty of faded, run-down, even dangerous places in town.

Those were the places she wanted to see, now. The dark side, the ugly shadow cast by the clean, pleasant, shining face that was all most people knew of Sunnydale. Seedy didn't even begin to describe some of it, but it was not all like that. Some of the areas were just poor. Gray and drab and filled with sadness.

Faith felt drawn to those places, wanted to understand them. They were familiar to her.

This was the third time in as many weeks that Faith had paused in her wandering to stand at the chain link fence and watch the elementary-school children at recess. They laughed and screamed and played and fought and fell down, the boys ran from the girls, then the girls ran away giggling. Some of the older kids, maybe fifth grade, seemed to hang out mostly at the edge of a small paved area under a basketball hoop with a drooping, ragged net. The first time she'd seen them, this knot of semi-tough, semi-popular-looking boys and girls, they'd been teasing the new kid.

Even now, Faith could see the girl they'd been making fun of that day. A pale little thing with short, shabbily-trimmed black hair, she sat on the other side of the lot, leaning against the brick building, and stared around the schoolyard at everyone and no one, almost daring anyone to speak to her.

They'd frozen the new girl out, and more than likely, out was where she would stay the rest of her life. *If she's lucky,* Faith thought, *maybe it will only be for the rest of fifth grade.*

The little clique under the basketball net was focused on each other today. Bickering about something one of the boys had supposedly said to one of the girls, some imagined insult or other, a rift had begun to form over who backed up whom, who believed which side of the story.

Faith watched them and felt like the sight of it should make her smile with appreciation for the irony; the scene reminded her so much of the people *she* knew in Sunnydale.

But, somehow, it wasn't funny at all.

Less than two months had passed since the debacle with Mrs. Post, and it seemed as though somewhere some cosmic force had been toying with them all. Given some of the things that had come to pass, Faith had to wonder if that were true.

On Christmas Eve, Angel had been haunted by an ancient evil that preyed upon his guilty feelings until he was ready to kill himself, to stand in the full light of Christmas morning's dawn and simply burn. But he did not burn, for that morning, it snowed in Sunnydale for the first time any of the locals could remember. They all saw it as intervention by some greater force, by the Powers That Be, to let Angel know he had a purpose.

Faith was envious. Buffy had been chosen as the Slayer. She was a Slayer, too, but her calling had been nothing more than accident. Coincidence. She wondered, very often, if the world needed more than one. Buffy did it so well, and she had her friends around to back her up.

Her friends.

Though she and Buffy had made amends since the strain that Mrs. Post's deception had put on them, it had never been quite the same since then. Faith knew that no matter what happened, she wasn't really one of them, wasn't really a part of the family that Buffy had. In a way, Faith had never been a part of *any* family, and it pained her. Here was this group of people so loyal to one another, and she could not be a part of it, no matter what she did.

On the other hand, Buffy's little family had been falling apart lately. Giles had been fired as her Watcher but continued *de facto* until another was appointed. Willow and Xander had been abducted by the vampire, Spike. In the heat of the moment, driven by their fear, they had started kissing. Faith could totally understand the urge. The problem was, they both were involved with other people, Willow with Oz and Xander with Cordelia.

And it was Oz and Cordelia who had gone to their rescue, walked in on them kissing. Eventually, Oz had forgiven Willow. That was the kind of guy he was. But Cordelia didn't have that in her. She had dropped Xander like he was on fire, barely even spoke to him now.

A free man. And he was part of Buffy's little family . . . and more than a little attractive, for a sidekick. During the nail-biting days in which Faith helped Giles, Buffy and the others to avert the apocalypse by defeating the demonic Sisterhood of Jhe, Faith had run into Xander at exactly the wrong—or maybe right—time. She had been wound up, anxious, and humming with the kind of energy she always got from a Slayerish workout.

She and Xander had gotten physical. *Very* physical. As far as Faith was concerned, it was just another example of the little splinters that kept developing in the little family that surrounded Buffy.

In the schoolyard, the group of fifth graders split up for real, stalking angrily away from each other in twos and threes. Faith watched them for a long moment, but then the school bell rang. As the children hurried back inside, Faith turned and continued on her way.

She put one foot in front of the other, going on instinct alone, and she had no idea where she was going to end up.

BAD GIRLS

CHAPTER 1

"**U**ngghh!" Faith grunted, as the vampire she was fighting cracked her hard across the face, snapping her out of her thoughts.

All right, she thought as she backhanded the drooling bloodsucker, *you got my attention*.

She had asked Buffy about it, about her and Xander, and Buffy had denied that she had ever been involved with him. Which Faith just couldn't buy.

With a flurry of blows, she beat the vampire back. Then she made the mistake of glancing at Buffy, and the big, hideous freak got the drop on her. Almost simultaneously, the one Buffy was fighting grabbed her around the throat. The two Slayers were slammed back to the ground, side by side, being throttled by the pair of vampires above them, trying to stay alive.

Even then, Faith's mind was on something else.

"So, what, you're telling me never?" she demanded.

"Faith, really," Buffy grunted, struggling with the vamp on top of her. "Now is not the time."

"I'm curious," Faith said defensively. "Never ever?"

As if they were one person, Faith and Buffy both flipped the vampires off them. They were old creatures, obvious from their medieval fashion sense. Both Slayers leaped up and were ready for more.

"Come on, really. All this time and not even once?" Faith asked incredulously.

One of the vamps rushed her, and Faith slugged it once, then tossed it onto the ground.

"How many times do I have to say this?" Buffy replied. "I have never—" the other vampire rushed her, and she punched it "—done it—" spun into a high kick to drive it back against a crypt "—with Xander!" She staked it, and the vampire erupted into a cloud of dust.

Buffy turned to Faith. "He's just a friend."

"So," Faith argued, as she dropped down to dust her vamp. "What are friends for?" She stood up and walked toward Buffy. "I mean, I'm sorry, it's just all the sweaty, nightly, side-by-side action, and you never put in for a little after hours—"

She grunted, made a little motion with her hips.

Buffy raised her eyebrows doubtfully. "Thanks for the poetry, and no. I love Xander, I just don't *love* Xander. Besides, I think it ruins friendships to do that stuff."

"You think too much," Faith told her.

But Buffy wasn't listening anymore. She was staring at a cluster of tracks and footprints in the dirt.

"There's one left," she said.

"How do you know?" Faith asked.

Buffy was deadly serious. "I think too much."

Quietly, she set off in the direction the tracks led. Faith followed, curious. Beyond a small tomb ahead, something moved in the dark. *Whaddaya know?* she thought. *Another one.*

"On three," Buffy whispered. "One—"

With a surge of adrenaline, Faith leaped up, rolled across the tomb, and came down on the other side. Sure enough, there was a third vampire there, wearing the same kind of ancient warrior garb that the others had worn.

"Three," she heard Buffy mutter behind her.

The vampire hit her once, but Faith parried, then launched a kick. The thing was faster than she'd expected, a better fighter. It caught her leg midkick and threw her hard to the ground.

Faith looked up to see Buffy—stake in hand—rush around the tomb at the vampire, but the warrior drew a pair of swords, one long and one short, from its belt. With the long sword, it hacked the stake in half. Buffy glanced at the useless weapon and threw it down. Then she attacked. With an expert combination of punches and kicks, she disarmed the vampire, its swords falling to the moldy ground.

But it was still powerful. Buffy struck it again, but the monster knocked her blows away and gripped her by the neck with both hands, strangling her. Buffy cried out.

Faith was there. Stake held high, she ran at the vampire, then punched the stake through its back and into the heart. It exploded into ashes that swirled in the breeze and were gone.

"Nicely diverted, B," Faith told her, and lifted her hand for a high five.

Buffy left her hanging. "Diverted," she replied, breathing hard. "That was me fighting for my life, Miss Attention Span."

"Hey, this isn't a Tupperware party. It's a little hard to plan."

"The count of three isn't a plan," Buffy snapped. "It's *Sesame Street*."

"Hey, they're toast and we're here, so it couldn't have

been too bad, right?" Faith reasoned. "Who were those guys, anyway?"

Buffy shrugged. "I don't know. They didn't seem local. Look, why don't we grab the weapons, maybe Giles . . ." Buffy's words trailed off as she looked over at the spot where the vampire had dropped his blades.

With a frown, Faith glanced over to see what had disturbed her so much.

The weapons were gone.

Mr. Trick had traded one employer for another. After Kakistos had been killed by the Slayers, he had wandered a bit but eventually took a job working for the Mayor of Sunnydale. In another town, that might have seemed strange, but not here. The Mayor seemed like a sweet, down-home America, Norman Rockwell old-fashioned kinda guy.

But he was also into some serious black arts, and he had a plan for some sort of personal Ascension that would give him unimaginable dark power.

Or something.

Trick never could quite figure it out. The guy had a tendency to talk in circles and not really share the full scope of his plan with those in his employ, including the nerdy Deputy Mayor, and Trick himself.

One of these days, Trick thought as he walked into the Mayor's office, the blades he'd picked up at the cemetery in his hands, *one of these days I'm gonna be the big boss instead of the lackey.*

Lackeying sucks.

The Mayor was reading the comic strips when Trick dropped the blades on his desk.

"Check these out," he said.

For a moment, the Mayor ignored him, giggling at the comics. "I just love *The Family Circus.* That P.J., he's getting to be quite a handful." He dropped the paper on his desk and examined the sword and dagger. "Well. I haven't seen anything like this in . . . well, a good long while. Where is the owner of these fine implements?"

"The common term is *slain*," Trick replied. "But I been seeing this breed around. Are we expecting any trouble?"

"Do you like *Family Circus?*" The Mayor asked.

"I like *Marmaduke*," Trick admitted.

"Oh, *euww*." The Mayor shuddered. "He's always on the furniture. Unsanitary."

"Nobody tellin' Marmaduke what to do. That's my kinda dog," Trick explained.

Allan, the nerdy Deputy Mayor, spoke up nervously. "I like to read *Cathy*."

Trick and the Mayor both glared at him.

"So what about these swords?" he asked, swallowing hard. "What should we do about that?"

"Let's just keep an eye out," the Mayor said grimly. "We've got the dedication coming up in a few days. We certainly can't have anything interfering with that."

"Well," Allan ventured, "maybe we should postpone the dedication?"

The Mayor paled, and stared at the Deputy Mayor.

"I believe the honorable Mayor hates that idea," Trick observed.

"The dedication," the Mayor said, rising from his desk and striding across the room, "is the final step before my Ascension. I have waited longer than you can imagine for this. After the hundred days, I'll be on a higher plane."

He opened a cabinet, inside which were talismans and skulls and objects of magickal power . . . and a box of tissues. He took one out and wiped his hands with it.

"And I'll have no more need for . . . well, let's just say I won't be concerned with the little things." He wadded up the tissue and handed it to Allan, who took it without hesitation. The Mayor walked back toward his desk. "Mr.

122 BUFFY THE VAMPIRE SLAYER

Trick, watch these people. Anything you find out about
them, well, let's just see that information reaches the
Slayers."

"Who knows?" he said, almost gleeful again. "With
any luck, they'll kill each other, and then everyone's a
winner. *Everyone*, of course, being me."

The Mayor giggled.

CHAPTER 2

During free period the next day, Buffy sat with Xander, Willow and Oz in the student lounge, and marveled over Willow's bevy of possible college choices. Xander sifted through college catalogs and large manila envelopes in amazement.

"Willow, what are these?" he asked.

"They're early admission packets."

"Harvard, Yale, Wesleyan . . . some German Polytechnical Institute whose name I can't pronounce." Xander sat back onto the bench and pointed at the packets as though they were contagious. "Is anyone else intimidated? Because I'm just expecting thin slips of paper with the words *no way* written in crayon."

Oz regarded him coolly. "They're typing those now."

"I'm so overwhelmed," Willow squealed with excitement. "I got in! To actual colleges. And they're wooing me . . . they're pitching woo."

Buffy smiled at her. "The wooing stage is always fun."

"But it's weird," Willowed countered. "Rejection I can handle 'cause of the years of training, but this . . ."

"I feel your pain, Will," Xander said with a cynical nod. "Like, right now? I'm torn between the fast-growing fields of appliance repair and motel management. Of course, I'm still waiting to hear back from the Corndog Emporium, so—"

"Well, I think it's great," Buffy said. "Early admission. Now there's nothing standing between you and a brilliant future."

Oz leaned forward. "If I may suggest? Graduate. Getting left back? Not the thrill ride you'd expect."

Even as he spoke, Cordelia strutted over. Buffy noticed that she was dressing to look hotter than ever, in a short black skirt and tight red top. After what had happened with Xander and Willow, it was not enough for Cordelia to dump him, she had to make him suffer for it every possible moment.

"That's so cute," she told him as she stepped up to them. "Planning life as a loser? Most people just turn out that way, but you're really taking charge."

"The comedy stylings of Cordelia Chase, everyone!" Xander said, a little too loud, a little too lounge-lizard. "Who, incidentally, won't be needing a higher education when she markets her own very successful line of Hooker Wear."

"Well, Xander, I could dress more like you, but . . . oh, *my* father has a job."

With that, she spun on one heel and marched off.

"I'm not gonna waste the perfect comeback on you now, but don't think I don't have it. Oh yes, its time will come." He turned and gazed desperately at his friends. "So, life beyond high school. Anyone. Please. Chime in."

"I hear it's nice," Buffy replied. "And a place I'll never go if I don't pass Mrs. Taggart's chem test tomorrow."

"Oh, I can help," Willow assured her. "Chemistry's easy. It's just like witchcraft, only less newt. So what do you say? Study jam, my house, tonight?"

"I'm there," Buffy vowed.

The bell rang and they all rose to head off to class. Buffy, however, wasn't in a rush to get to class. She had other work to do.

"I have to go see Giles. Report on last night's patrol."

"Oh, yeah, he said he wanted to talk to you."

"What about? Is he okay?" Buffy asked, concerned.

Willow frowned. "He's looked better."

In the library, Giles was at the end of his rope, lingering somewhere between bored to death and on the verge of homicide. For the sake of propriety and simple courtesy, and his position with the Council, he was attempting to be polite. But that was not easy when it came to the slender, stuffy, annoying man who even now was poking about in his rare books.

This new arrival was more than a bit full of himself. *Thinks he's Sean Connery when he's quite a bit more George Lazenby,* Giles thought. An amusing comparison, but it gave him only a moment's good humor. Very little would relieve the throb in his skull at the moment, other than perhaps kicking Wesley out of the library on his bony ass. But he could not do that. He was no longer Buffy's Watcher, after all.

Wesley was.

"Of course, training procedures have been updated quite a bit since your day," Wesley said superciliously. "Much greater emphasis on field work."

"Really?" Giles asked, voice droll.

"Oh yes. It's not all books and theory nowadays. I have in fact faced two vampires myself. Under controlled circumstances, of course."

"You're in no danger of finding those here," Giles informed him.

"Vampires?"

"Controlled circumstances. Hello, Buffy," he said, as she entered the library.

She checked out Wesley with more than a little suspicion in her gaze.

"Well, hello," he said, attempting to be dashing.

Buffy glanced at Giles. "New Watcher?"

"New Watcher," he confirmed.

Wesley stepped toward her and thrust out his hand. "Wesley Wyndam-Pryce. It's very nice to meet you."

With a downward tick of her eyes, Buffy took in Wesley's hand, but ignored it. A bit put off, he backed off slightly.

The Slayer looked at Giles again. "Is he evil?"

"Evil?" Wesley asked, taken aback.

"The last one was evil," Buffy informed him.

"Oh yes," Wesley said, lifting his chin. "Gwendolyn Post. We all heard. Mr. Giles has checked my credentials rather thoroughly and phoned the Council, but I'm glad to see you're on the ball as well." He leaned in toward her with more than a bit of melodrama. "A good Slayer is a cautious Slayer."

Dubious, Buffy glanced at Giles again. "Is he evil?"

"Not in the strictest sense," the Watcher replied.

"Well, I'm glad that's cleared up," Wesley sniffed, obviously a bit peeved. "And as I'm sure none of us is anxious to waste time on pleasantries, why don't you tell me everything about last night's patrol."

Bored, Buffy rolled her eyes. "Vampires."

"Yes?" Wesley prodded.

"Killed 'em."

"Anything else you can tell me?"

Giles understood her reluctance but he gave her a look

that encouraged her to continue. She did so only grudgingly.

"One of them had swords. I don't think he was with the other two."

Wesley's eyes lit up. "Swords?" He hurried to a box of books he had brought with him from London, and flipped the pages of one near the top. "One long, one short?"

Buffy nodded. "Both pointy. With jewels and stuff."

"Sounds familiar," Giles noted.

"It should," Wesley informed him. He handed Giles the book, open to a page with lavish illustrations of a pair of ancient swords.

"El Eliminati," Giles began to read.

Wesley cut him off. "Fifteenth-century duelist cult. Deadly in their day, their numbers dwindled in later centuries due to an increase in anti-vampire activity and a lot of pointless dueling. They eventually became the acolytes of a demon called Balthazar, who brought them to the New World. Specifically, here."

Giles closed the book and handed it back to him. "You seem to know a lot about them."

Smug, Wesley returned the book to the box. "I didn't get this job because of my looks."

"I really really believe that," Buffy chirped amiably.

"I've researched this town's history," Wesley retorted, obviously stung. "Extensively."

"So why haven't we seen them before this?" Giles inquired.

"They were driven out a hundred years ago. Happily, Balthazar was killed. I don't know by whom."

"And . . . they're back 'cause?"

"Balthazar had an amulet, purported to give him strength. When he was killed, it was taken by a wealthy landowner named . . . I don't want to bore you with the details—"

Buffy raised one eyebrow. "Little bit late."

"—named Gleaves. It was buried with him and I believe the few remaining Eliminati are probably looking for it. For sentimental value."

Something about that sounded off to Giles. "And you don't think this amulet poses any threat?"

"Oh no, not at all. Nonetheless, we may as well keep it from them. Buffy, you will go to the Gleaves family crypt tonight and fetch the amulet," Wesley proclaimed.

Buffy smirked. "I will?"

The new Watcher frowned. "Are you not used to being given orders?"

"Whenever Giles sends me on a mission, he always says *please,*" Buffy said brightly. "And afterward, I get a cookie!" Beside her, Giles stifled a chuckle.

"I don't feel we're getting off on quite the right foot," Wesley began.

He was interrupted when Faith pushed through the library doors. She swaggered in, dragging one finger along the book checkout counter.

"Ah!" Wesley said appreciatively. "This is perhaps Faith?"

Faith checked him out top to bottom, a look close to disgust on her features. She glanced toward Buffy and Giles. "New Watcher?"

"New Watcher," they confirmed in unison.

"Screw that." She turned and strode back out of the library.

Petulant, Buffy looked at Giles. "Now why didn't I just say that?"

"Buffy, could you—" Giles began. He didn't even have to finish.

"I'll see if I can get her back," Buffy sighed. She got up and walked past Wesley. "Don't say anything incredibly interesting while I'm gone."

Together, the two men watched her go. When the doors swung shut, Wesley nodded once.

"They'll get used to me."

Outside, Buffy caught up to Faith as she stormed across the quad, not far from the fountain.

"Faith, wait," she said, moving up beside her. Faith stopped reluctantly and regarded Buffy. "I know this new guy's a dork, but . . . actually, I have nothing to follow that. He's just a dork."

"You're actually gonna take orders from him?" Faith replied, almost sneering. The prospect seemed absurd.

Buffy shrugged. "That's the job. What else can we do?"

"Whatever we want," Faith enthused. "We're Slayers, girlfriend. The Chosen Two. Why should we let him take all the fun out of it?"

"That'd be tragic. Taking the fun out of slaying, stabbing, beheading—"

"Oh, like you don't dig it?"

"I don't," Buffy argued.

"You're a liar," Faith jabbed. "I've seen you. Tell me staking a vamp doesn't get you a little bit juiced. Come on, say it."

A bit embarrassed, Buffy glanced away. People passed by them, walking around the fountain.

Faith laughed gently. "You can't fool me. The look in your eyes right after a kill? Just get hungry for more."

"You are way off base," Buffy told her.

"Tell me that if you don't get in a good slaying, after a while you start itching for a vamp to show up so you can give him a good *ungghh!*" Faith thrust out her hand as though she held a stake.

"Again with the grunting," Buffy pointed out. "You realize I'm not comfortable with this."

Faith threw her hands up, a bright, cajoling smile on

her face. "Hey, slaying's what we were built for. If you're not enjoying it, you're doing something wrong." She turned to walk away.

"What about the assignment?" Buffy called after her.

Faith paused only for a moment. "Tell you what, you do the homework, and I'll copy yours."

Night birds hooted and a cool breeze blew leaves across the grass as Buffy walked through Shady Hill Cemetery late that night. She had a flashlight in hand, but it gave her little comfort. Though she was the Slayer, and ready for anything, she preferred her foes to be right in front of her. As she approached the crypt, however, a chill ran up her back and she could not push away the feeling that there were eyes upon her, that something sinister lurked nearby.

With a shudder, she pushed the heavy door of the crypt open with a creak and stepped inside. The flashlight beam illuminated the stone tombs and drawers, the sculpted statues. It was an enormous crypt. The Gleaves family had been very wealthy.

Wonder who got all the money, she thought idly. *'Cause it sure looks like everybody who ever had the name Gleaves is right here.*

Tentatively, she moved to the first of the stone coffins. The tomb's heavy lid seemed to stick a bit as she tried to slide it off, and then suddenly it moved with a rasp of stone on stone. She shone the flashlight inside, and it illuminated the moldering bones within. There was no amulet.

"Strike one," she muttered softly.

Quickly, wanting to be gone, she moved to the next tomb and forced the slab of stone to one side. When she flashed the light within, its glow glimmered off a jeweled amulet that was strung around the neck of a dusty corpse in red robes.

"Game over," Buffy said to herself, more than a bit relieved.

Then she heard voices behind her. She spun and saw the flickering of torches as someone approached the tomb. A lot of someones.

Without the amulet, she leaped back to the first tomb and dropped inside, next to moldy, bare bones. She snapped the flashlight off and dragged the slab across above her, closing herself inside with the skeleton.

Then she waited.

She could hear footsteps. A lot of foosteps. The guttering torchlight was barely visible through cracks in the stone. A clinking of metal told her she had failed in her mission. They had the amulet.

A moment later they went out again, the light of the torches and the sound of their footsteps receding. Buffy counted to ten and pushed back the stone slab above her. She rose up from the tomb . . . and felt a strong hand suddenly grip her shoulder.

Gasping, she turned to see a familiar face. "Faith!"

"What are you doing, hiding in there?"

"Looking for the amulet," Buffy said defensively. "Wasn't counting on the special guest stars, six against one. Hence the hiding."

Faith nodded. "Six against two, now, so come on."

Outside, they saw the last of the vampires, torch in hand, drop into a sewer manhole and disappear. Faith rushed toward the hole in the ground, right in the middle of the cemetery.

"Wait. Stop. Think." Buffy chased after her.

"No. No. No." Faith kept going.

"It's a manhole. Tight space, no escape, six against two—not unlike three against one," Buffy reminded her.

"And there might be more," Faith replied. "So come on."

"You're just gonna go down there? That's your plan?" Buffy asked, stupefied.

"Who said I had a plan?" Faith countered. "I don't know how many's down there, but I wanna find out, and I'll know when I land. And if you don't come in after me—" Faith stepped up next to the manhole and smiled. "I might die."

Faith jumped in without a second's hesitation.

Buffy rolled her eyes and stared at the manhole for a second.

Then she jumped in after her.

CHAPTER 3

In the library, Giles paced anxiously, wondering why Buffy had not yet returned from the Gleaves crypt. At the study table, Wesley sat flipping through stacks of books, some of which were handwritten: the journals of the Watchers.

"These are all the diaries, then? Yours included?" he asked.

"That's everything," Giles replied. "Knock yourself out. Please."

Wesley flipped through Giles's journal. "Oh, yes. Here's your first entry. 'Slayer is willful and insolent.' That would be our girl, wouldn't it?"

Giles was not amused. "You have to get to know her."

Wesley went on reading. " 'Her abuse of the English language is such that I understand only every other sentence.' This is going to make fascinating reading."

Impatient and anxious, Giles glanced at his watch. "She should be back by now."

Dubiously, Wesley took a quick look at his own watch.

"Not to fret," he cautioned Giles, as he grabbed a licorice from a small jar on the table and popped it into his mouth. "My mission scenario has her back in one minute. Shouldn't be any trouble."

Crack!
Faith launched a high kick at the vampire in front of her, and felt its cheek give way under the blow. He stumbled backward, clutching his face in pain. Beside her, Buffy pummeled a second vamp with such force that he was nearly driven off his feet. But there were more of them. Too many, just like Buffy had said.

Beautiful, Faith thought. *Bring it on.* It was just what she needed, and she believed it was just what Buffy needed as well, whether the other Slayer knew it or not.

They were in a spacious sewer maintenance area, where various tunnels ended and others began, and where shutoff valves would allow control of the flow of some pipes in the area. But in the months she'd spent in town, Faith had learned that there were other tunnels that also led into the place, rough hewn out of the earth. Beneath Sunnydale was a warren of tunnels, both man- and demon-made. This was one of the places where the two came together.

Demon Junction, Faith thought.
All the vampires were swordsmen like the one they had killed the night before, but not all of them had their blades out. Faith figured they were having the same problem she and Buffy were faced with. The fight was so fast and furious they had time mainly to defend themselves, and no time to pull out a stake and finish anyone off. With every blow that fell, every vampire they backhanded or kicked away, another was right in front of them. There were only six of them, but they were fast, and expert fighters.

"We're surrounded!" Buffy snapped at Faith.

"Oh, you noticed that, too?" Faith replied with a little laugh.

Buffy did a spinning kick that took a vamp in the face. She planted her feet, then kicked him in the gut. Another swept down upon her with his blade and she dodged just in time. The metal bit into cold concrete instead of hot flesh.

Across the junction, Faith flipped one hard into the wall and it grunted in pain. She turned as another rushed her, and she kicked him backward. Both Slayers threw punches right and left, but Faith was barely able to keep track of the faces of the monsters around her, just striking out at everything that approached her. She was a whirlwind. Fists and feet flying, her heart racing madly, bone and flesh giving way under her blows.

It was exhilarating, a high like nobody else in the world could ever understand. Except Buffy. If only Buffy would just let herself go, let it flow.

Two broad-shouldered vamps moved in quickly, took her while she was defending herself from a third, and slammed her against the wall. Faith was pinned. Eyes wild as she struggled with them, she looked over at Buffy, who had managed to clear the space around her. There were three vampires on the ground by her, recovering, preparing for another attack. Buffy whipped out a stake. She would have time to dust at least one of them, and Faith was not about to distract her. She could take care of herself.

But then Buffy glanced over and saw Faith's predicament. Without hesitation, she threw the stake. End over end, it flew through the air and punctured the back of one of the vamps pinning Faith to the wall. The vampire shouted in pain, then exploded into ash.

The eyes of the two Slayers met. Faith offered Buffy a tiny smile. *Now you're getting into it,* she thought.

Then, before Faith could shout a warning, she saw a vampire attack Buffy from behind and grab her in a painful hold, both arms behind her back. Faith called out to her, but more vampires were upon her in an instant, and she beat them back, trying to get to Buffy. A vamp got in her way and she head-butted him so she could get a clear look.

A second vampire had approached Buffy now, long and short swords drawn, the amulet they had been searching for tucked into his belt. He pointed the long sword at Buffy's chest.

"Let's settle this honorably," he said.

As Faith backhanded a vamp in front of her, she caught the rest of the action in quick glimpses. Buffy kicked the long sword from the vampire's hand and it landed in a concrete catching pool beside her, splashing down into the water. She threw off the vamp holding her, but the one with the amulet, angry, grabbed her throat and thrust the shorter blade at her gut. Buffy dodged, and held onto his wrist.

"Then let's just settle it," the vampire snarled. He pushed her over the edge of the catching pool and shoved her head under, attempting to drown her.

As she hammered at the vampires around her, Faith screamed Buffy's name. She saw Buffy struggle against the vampire's grip, but her movements slowed quickly. Then she stopped moving altogether. After a moment, he released her and turned away. Buffy only lay there.

Faith thundered her name and lashed out with a kick that shattered bone, then spun and lunged, using a palm strike to break the nose of the vampire in front of her. It staggered back. Faith turned to bolt toward the pool of water, intent upon saving Buffy somehow.

But Buffy didn't need saving. As Faith watched, her seemingly-dead form twitched, her hand reached out, and her fingers closed upon the hilt of the vampire's long sword. Buffy surged from the water, sword already in motion, coming down to hack off the head of the vamp with the amulet.

He dodged.

"I hate when they drown me," Buffy noted, almost casually.

Faith laughed gleefully, feeling the energy that seemed to crackle between them. *This is what we were built for!*

The vampire brought up the short sword but Buffy swung her own blade and knocked it from his hand. A vamp grabbed Faith by the arm, forced her up against the wall again, but she shook loose, struck him twice, and tossed him into one of the sewer tunnels.

But there were a lot more where he came from. It was fun while it had lasted, but Faith had to admit to herself that Buffy had been right all along. There were just too many of them.

"B!" Faith snapped. "Gotta go!"

"We came for the amulet," Buffy replied. She thrust out the sword, using it to pluck the amulet from the vampire's belt.

Realizing the Slayers now had the upper hand, the vampire turned to run after the one Faith had tossed into the tunnel, and the others were taking off too. Faith grinned. All of a sudden, they had overcome the odds against them.

Heart still racing, Faith strutted to Buffy's side with a broad grin. "Tell me you don't get off on this."

Buffy held the amulet in her hand and examined it. A tiny half-smile played on her lips. "Didn't suck."

That's my girl, Faith thought. *That's what we are. Two of a kind.*

It was not until the following morning that Buffy reported to Giles . . . and reluctantly to Wesley, since he was actually her Watcher now. The previous night she and Faith had called it quits after their vampire marathon. She was tired this morning, but in an odd way, Buffy had never felt better.

In the library, Wesley turned the amulet over in his hands and studied it, holding it up so close that Buffy thought he was going to kiss it.

"Well, looks authentic enough," he proclaimed, setting it down. "Of course, there are tests to be made before actual verification."

Buffy frowned. "How about verifying that your 'nearly extinct' cult was out in magnum force last night? Faith and I got into a serious party situation."

Giles stood in the doorway to his inner office. "Are you all right?" he asked, his concern plain.

"I had to lather, rinse and repeat about five million times to get the sewer out of my hair, but otherwise, I'm of the good," she replied. "Thank *you* for asking." Buffy shot a meaningful look at Wesley.

Wesley ignored the barb. "Perhaps there were a few more than we'd anticipated, but I'd expect you to be ready for anything. Remember the three key words for any Slayer. Preparation. Preparation. Preparation."

"That's one word three times," Buffy told him, openly challenging him now.

The school bell rang.

"I have a chem test," the Slayer said, rising. "It's so sad that I'm actually happy about that." As she walked toward the door, she glanced at the man she would always think of as her Watcher, no matter who the Council sent. "Giles, we need to talk."

Wesley bristled. "Buffy, I must ask you to remember that I am your Watcher. From now on, anything you have to say about slaying, you will say to me. The only thing you need discuss with Mr. Giles is overdue book fees. Understood?"

With a sigh, Buffy turned to Giles again. "We'll talk."

"Of course," he agreed.

Late already, she walked out. As she left, she overheard Wesley chide him.

"You're not helping," the new Watcher said sternly.

"I know," Giles mused. "I feel just sick about it."

By the time she sat in the chem lab waiting for the test to start, Buffy had forgotten all about how annoying Wesley was. Her mind was on the night before, and how pumped she'd been during the fight with the sword-wielding vampires. Willow and Xander sat at the lab table behind her, and Buffy was turned around in her seat. She was trying to explain how it felt, but didn't think she was really communicating it well.

"It was intense," she told Willow. "It was like I just let go and I became this force. I just didn't care anymore."

"Yeah, I know what that's like," Willow replied.

"I don't think you can," Buffy told her. "It's kind of a Slayer thing. I don't even think I'm explaining it well."

"You're explaining it a *lot*, though," Xander told her.

Mrs. Taggart slipped their test booklets in front of them, then walked to the front of the class.

"All right. You have one period to fill out your test booklets. Periodic tables are located on the back, and you're on the honor system, so remember . . . no talking."

The second Mrs. Taggart looked away, Buffy turned back to Willow. "The thing was, Faith knew that I didn't even want to go down there—"

At the front of the room, the teacher cleared her throat. Buffy turned to look at her.

"Miss Summers?"

Buffy made the lock-it-and-throw-away-the-key gesture at her lips. Mrs. Taggart nodded once, then regarded the entire class.

"You have one hour," she told them. Then she went out and pulled the door shut behind her.

Without even another glance at the door, Buffy turned back to Willow. "Okay, so the best part—"

"Buffy, test?" Willow interrupted. "Y'know, remember? The thing you didn't come over to study for."

"Right, got it. Sorry," Buffy told her. Then she moved closer to Xander. "Okay, so we're down there, in the sewers, and Faith's got three of them on her at once—"

"Hey, whoa!" Xander stopped her. "Can we resume Buffy's ode to Faith later? Like when I'm not actively multiple-choicing?"

Buffy stared at him for a second. "How come your eye twitches every time I say Faith's name?"

Even as she said it, his eye twitched again. "What? No it doesn't."

She leaned in, staring at him. "Faith."

Xander's eye twitched and he slapped a hand over it. "Cut it out. We've got a test to take and I'm highly caffeinated, and I'm trying to concentrate. Some of us actually care about school, you know."

Buffy was far from convinced. But when Xander went back to his test, she didn't bug him again. She glanced around the class and saw that everyone was hard at work on their booklets—except her. Buffy did not want to take the test. She did not want to be in school at all. Bored, she looked around.

As if summoned, Faith knocked at the window, grinning as she looked inside. She hauled the window open and stuck her head in.

"Hey, girlfriend," Faith said. "Bad time?" She breathed on the window and drew a tiny heart in the condensation, and an arrow through it.

Clever, Buffy thought. It was a love symbol for some. To them, it meant something completely different. Or maybe not completely, not the way slaying was making Buffy feel lately.

She got up and headed for the window.

"No, she can't!" Willow said quickly. "You can't, can you?"

Buffy climbed out through the window. Faith closed it behind her, and then they were out in the sun, striding across the high school grounds, and she felt better than she had all morning.

"What's up?" she asked.

Faith nodded once, nonchalantly. "Vampires."

"Uh, Faith, unless there's a total eclipse in the next five minutes? It's daylight."

"Good for us, bad for them. I found a nest."

Buffy smiled. "That has potential."

Fifteen minutes later, they reached the abandoned building Faith had identified as a squat for vampires. The windows were boarded up or painted over.

As one, they kicked down the double doors in front. The Slayers entered with a crash, and the sweet yet brutal sun poured in behind them. Vampires were strewn like garbage over the floor, sleeping the day away like junkies in a crack house. When the sunlight streamed in, at least two of them caught fire and began to scream.

The others scrambled and ran.

"Rise and shine, people," Faith said.

Buffy watched them run, and grinned. "This is your wake-up call."

Emotion washed through Faith. Or maybe it wasn't emotion. Maybe it was just adrenaline. Whatever it was, she liked it. Night had fallen outside and she and Buffy were in the Bronze. The electronic rhythms moved through her, pulsating through her body as she danced with Buffy. In all the world there were only the two of them. Though they had had their differences, Faith could tell that Buffy was beginning to see that Faith's philosophy was one of freedom.

Freedom felt amazing.

Wild, she shook her hips and moved, swaying crazily. Compared to Buffy, Faith's dancing was more out of control, like she could slip the reins of whatever might have held her back, and just allow her primal self to move to the music. Faith could sense that Buffy envied her ability to do that. She was in the process of becoming a wild thing, and there was something wonderful about that. But she wasn't quite there yet.

Not like Faith.

They danced together, and they drew guys like flies to honey. The guys started to flock around them, but Buffy and Faith kept their focus on each other. They were celebrating the vampire nest they'd cleaned out that day, and the celebration was just for themselves.

Buffy glanced across the Bronze and saw Angel watching her, grim-faced. She slipped away from Faith and the guys and ran to him. She leaped up into his arms and wrapped her legs around him.

"Hey. You're not leaving, are you?" she asked.

"Saw you making friends," he replied.

"Them?" Buffy asked, heat surging up within her. "Boys. I like *you*."

Angel let her down and she stood looking up at him.

"What's the matter? You're not afraid of little me, are you?"

"We better sit down." Angel drew her behind him by the hand and they found a sofa in the back.

"I can sense this is a business trip," Buffy sighed. "What's the what?"

"Balthazar," Angel revealed.

Buffy wrapped her arms around him. "Dead demon."

"Not as dead as you think," he replied. He stood up and moved to another couch, across from her. "Word on the street puts him in the packing warehouse on Devereau. He's looking for—"

"His amulet. It's supposed to restore his strength."

"From what I'm hearing, that's not something we'd like to see happen."

Buffy smiled. "No problem. We've got the amulet."

"I know," Angel responded. "I spoke to Giles, but he said you gave it to—"

Wesley poked his head around the corner. "Ah, there you are!"

"Wow, speak of the really annoying person," Buffy said happily.

"You're certainly giving me a run for my money," Wesley replied, glancing around in distaste at the Bronze. He sat down beside her and spoke in a whisper, apparently so that Angel would not hear. "I think we should establish that if you're going to go out slaying, you leave me a number where I can contact you."

Angel wasn't patient. "Where's the amulet?"

Startled, Wesley looked at him. "Who are you?"

"A friend," Buffy said. "Do you have it?"

"It's somewhere very safe," Wesley said pompously.

Buffy frowned, then took a close look at him. Rolling her eyes, she reached inside his jacket and pulled the amulet out of the inner pocket.

"How did you know?"

"Pooches your jacket." She tossed the amulet to Angel.

Wesley gaped. "Now, hang on a minute."

"Walking around with this thing is like wearing a target," Angel warned him.

"You'll put it somewhere safe that's actually safe?" Buffy asked.

Angel rose from the couch. "I'll do it now."

Buffy got up as well. "I'll do some recon on Balthazar."

Looking a bit like a spoiled child about to have a tantrum, Wesley stood up and barred Buffy's way. "If I may, Balthazar is dead. Am I the only one who remembers that?"

"Be careful," Angel cautioned her, then leaned in for a quick kiss.

"You know me," she replied sassily.

He eyed her warily. "I mean it."

Angel headed for the door and Buffy walked back out on the dance floor, leaving Wesley to glance around in utter confusion. On the floor, Faith was grinding provocatively with a pair of cute guys. As Buffy passed by, she grabbed Faith by the hand and pulled her away.

"Call me!" Faith told the guys.

In a rented warehouse on Devereau Street, in Sunnydale's commercial district, the night was just beginning. The demon Balthazar sat in his bathing tank, sickeningly pale skin constantly moistened by his vampire slaves, who ladled water from the tank onto him. Though at well over one thousand pounds, Balthazar could barely move his enormous bulk, he felt the power that raced through him and knew that he was truly magnificent.

And, at the moment, he was also enraged.

His jellylike flesh quivered as he snarled at the Eliminati swordsmen arrayed before him.

"Let me tell you what I see," he rasped at them. "I see fear. And remorse. And the pitiful look of faces that cry out for mercy. What I don't see is what I want to see, and that's my amulet!"

"Lord Balthazar," one of them replied, terrified. "We found it. We had it! But the Slayers—"

"Already I'm bored," Balthazar snapped.

With the power inside him, Balthazar reached out.

Mystical energy allowed him to move objects by sheer will alone. His size kept him from moving much, but it mattered not when he could bring anything to him. The vampire was yanked off his feet and flew into Balthazar's hands. The demon crushed his servant's head with a satisfying crackle.

Balthazar glanced up at the commander of the remaining Eliminati. "Vincent, come here," he said.

Reluctantly, Vincent moved toward him.

"Closer. Closer," Balthazar urged. When Vincent was leaning over the bathing tank, Balthazar laid a hand on his shoulder. "Let me tell you what I want to see."

Outside the warehouse, Faith and Buffy watched all of this through a broken window.

"Okay, we got ten, maybe twelve bad guys," Buffy said quietly. "And one big demon in desperate need of a Stairmaster."

No problem.

"I say we take 'em all, hard and fast, now!" Faith urged.

Buffy glanced at her. Faith knew that only days before, Buffy would have insisted they have a better plan than that. But Faith's recklessness was rubbing off on her.

"We need a little more firepower than none. We should head back to the library," Buffy reasoned.

"Well, I guess Jacuzzi Boy isn't going anywhere," Faith allowed, glancing around at the other buildings on the street. "I just wish we had . . . oh, that is too good."

Buffy followed her line of vision. Across the street she spotted Meyer Sports & Tackle. Faith set off toward the store, but Buffy hesitated. She knew instantly what Faith had in mind and it meant the difference between wild-at-heart and breaking-and-entering.

Of course, in the time it took them to go back to the library and return with weapons, Balthazar and El Eliminati might have taken lives. With that in the balance, Faith was sure Buffy couldn't argue with her methods.

Not that it would make a difference, Faith thought. It was too late to stop her, anyway.

Faith kicked in the door of the sporting goods store. Nervously, Buffy followed her inside. They strode quickly within, looking for weapons.

"Ooh, score," Faith said as she looked around excitedly.

With an elbow, Faith shattered a glass case and withdrew an expensive crossbow.

"Think they're insured?" Buffy asked tentatively.

Faith smirked. "Strangely, not my priority. When are you gonna get this, B? The life of a Slayer is very simple. Want . . ." Faith walked over to another glass case, filled with weapons, and put her fist through it. "Take." She reached in and pulled out a pair of nunchuks. "Have."

Buffy watched her, both amazed and a little impressed, in spite of herself. And they did need the weapons, after all. She turned and saw another case filled with impressive hunting and throwing knives.

"Want, take, have," she said in a low voice. Then she punched a fist through the case and withdrew the most dangerous-looking of the knives. "I'm getting it."

Faith kicked in another case and pulled out a huge compound bow with some arrows. *That's right, girlfriend.*

A gun went off.

Two policemen in uniform appeared, their service weapons leveled at her and Buffy.

"Drop the weapons and get down on the ground! Now!"

CHAPTER 4

Faith eyed the cops who had caught them, red-handed, in the middle of robbing the sporting goods store. Their guns wavered uncertainly in their grasps. She figured the last thing they had expected to find when they responded to the store's alarm was a couple of teenaged girls stealing compound bows and hunting knives.

Now what? Faith thought. Harsh reality: they had committed a crime, and the police were doing exactly what they were supposed to do. They would go to jail.

Not gonna happen. No way was she going to jail. But she was not in the mood to take a bullet, either. She would have to bide her time.

"I said drop the weapons, or I fire," the older of the two cops said sternly. He took a step toward them, gun held steady in both hands.

Buffy tossed the knife she'd stolen to one side. After a moment's hesitation, Faith rolled her eyes and tossed the compound bow away from her.

"Now spread 'em!" the cop commanded.

"You wish," Faith sneered.

The officer twitched. "Hands in the air where I can see 'em," he instructed. "Slow," he added, when Faith moved a bit too quickly for his comfort level. Then he glanced at his partner. "Good. Cuff 'em."

As the younger officer pulled out his handcuffs and moved around behind them, Faith shot an amused glance at Buffy. "I like him," she said. "He's butch."

Buffy didn't seem to think it was at all funny.

Five minutes later, they were cruising through Sunnydale in the caged-in rear of a police patrol car, hands cuffed behind their backs. As the lights of downtown Sunnydale flashed across the darkened windshield, the policeman glanced in the rearview mirror and talked to them.

"That's some artillery you two were putting together. You with one of them girl gangs?" he asked.

"Yeah. We're the Slayers," Faith replied dryly. She considered their options. Then she turned to Buffy. "You want to get outta here?" She slid down in her seat and lifted her legs slightly, to indicate that she intended to kick away the metal caging that separated the front and rear of the car.

Buffy cast a dubious glance at Faith.

"Can't save the world in jail," Faith reminded her.

Slowly, with obvious reluctance, Buffy slid down beside her. Almost silently, Faith counted to three, and then the two of them kicked the metal mesh so that it snapped off its supports and slammed the two cops forward. Both of them struck their heads against the windshield and the driver lost control of the car.

Tires squealed and the driver swerved and crashed into a car parked at the edge of Hammersmith Park. Dogs began to bark loudly as the girls extricated themselves from the vehicle. Faith had managed to retrieve the handcuff keys, and they moved quickly back to back as she began attempting to unlock the cuffs.

"We should call an ambulance," Buffy said, staring at the unconscious cops in the front seat.

"Five people already have, the racket we made," Faith scolded her. "And they're fine."

As if on cue, the two officers began to come around, groaning. Faith unlocked the cuffs. "Come on, let's get out of here," she said, hustling away. "Come on!"

For a second, she was not sure if Buffy was going to follow. Then, with one reluctant glance at the cops, she did. Faith felt energized by the chaos, and she loved that Buffy was with her, breaking the rules. They were together, the two of them. A team at last.

The next morning, Buffy still had a sick feeling in her gut. When she stepped outside it was too bright, too sunny, almost as if the day were mocking the dark cloud that lingered over her from the night before. She grabbed the newspaper off the stoop and brought it back inside. At the kitchen table she opened it and leafed through the pages, searching for information about the cops from the night before, and hoping they had not come up with any way to identify her and Faith as the culprits.

Her mother stepped into the kitchen in a rumpled robe, looking like she was still half asleep.

"Admit it," Joyce said grumpily.

Buffy blinked, guilt surging through her, and turned to her mother.

"Some days don't you wanna just wake up and say to hell with the diet?" Joyce went on. "Wanna make waffles? Big Saturday brunch?"

"I'm not really that hungry," Buffy replied, and turned the page, eyes still on the paper.

Joyce sighed and crossed the kitchen and began to make a pot of coffee. "So what'd you and Faith do last night?"

"Nothing," Buffy said, a little too quickly. "Nothing really important."

"Don't worry. I'm not going to meddle in your slaying. Just as long as you're careful."

"I am," Buffy assured her, but without any confidence in her voice. She stared at the newspaper for a moment longer, then closed it.

"You sure about those waffles?"

"Yeah, but if you want them I can help you make them."

"No," her mother said sadly. "They only don't have calories if I make them for you. Mom logic." She reached for the paper. "You all done with this?"

Buffy nodded. "Yeah."

"Let's see what's happening in Sunnydale," Joyce said slowly.

The Mayor smiled broadly and put his arms around a couple of Boy Scouts. The whole troop was gathered around him as the photographer clicked the last of the pictures. The flash went off, and the Mayor patted a couple of the boys on the back.

"There we go. Thanks a lot, fellas," he said as the Deputy Mayor ushered them out the door. "Thanks a heap. Hey, have fun on that camping trip now. Don't forget to roast a wiener for me."

He walked around shutting the blinds as the Deputy Mayor shut the door behind the Boy Scouts. The Mayor chuckled to himself. When the last of the blinds had been pulled, he glanced at the door that led to a small office just off of his.

"All right, you can come out now."

The door opened immediately, and Mr. Trick entered.

"Backbone of America, those little guys," the Mayor declared, wagging a finger in the direction the Scouts had gone. "Seeing the hope and courage on their bright little faces, I swear I could just . . . I could just eat 'em up."

He strode across the room to the large cabinet in which he kept his arcane artifacts and the small shrine he had made to his demon masters, as well as his wet bar. "So, any news on the Eliminati?" he asked.

When he opened the cabinet doors, there was a snarl, and the leader of El Eliminati, Vincent, sprang from within. Savagely, he forced the Mayor back, threw him on top of his desk, and pointed his short sword at the Mayor's throat.

"In the name of Lord Balthazar, die!" Vincent growled.

Mr. Trick punched the vampire swordsman in the side of the head, driving him to the ground, unconscious.

The Mayor coughed a bit as he stood up and straightened his jacket and tie. "Thank you, Mr. Trick, that was very thoughtful of you."

Trick picked up Vincent's blade and handed it to the Deputy Mayor, who plucked it with two fingers as though it were the rotting carcass of some dead thing.

"Why do they always gotta be using swords?" Trick mused. "It's called an Uzi, chump. Woulda saved your ass right about now."

But the Mayor was paying no attention to Trick. His dark gaze had come to rest on the anxious Deputy Mayor. "Curious how he could have gotten all the way into my liquor cabinet. Allan, don't we have security working in this building?"

Allan stumbled over his words. "Sir, I . . . I have no idea."

"There's no need to swoon, Allan, but we're trying to keep things secure." The Mayor gestured toward the unconscious Eliminati attacker. "Lock him up."

Mr. Trick grunted. "He wakes up he's just gonna try and kill you again."

"Yes," the Mayor agreed as he sank down into the fine leather chair behind his desk. "Yes, I expect he will."

Once again, Balthazar's plans had been thwarted. Fury raged within him with such heat that he was surprised the waters in his bathing tank did not begin to boil. He glared at the Eliminati arrayed before him, and he hated them all. Yet he needed them as well.

"Vincent made a noble effort," he told them, seething. "Man to man, as befits a true warrior. He had courage. He had honor. *And I have jack to show for it!*"

He screamed this last, almost losing control completely. The demon breathed slowly, attempting to cool his fiery temper. His lackeys continued to use huge ladles to take water from the tank and pour over his rancid bulk, keeping his flesh moist.

"It has been a hundred years since my enemy crippled me," Balthazar snarled. "Now ultimate power is within his grasp, and I will not let it be! Forget about honor! Forget about everything but getting my amulet! Bring the Watchers to me! Find the Slayers and kill them! Kill everything that gets in your way. Go! *Go!*" he screamed.

The vampires ran, fleeing in terror, to perform the tasks he commanded.

Buffy sat in her bedroom with Willow. Her friend had given her a tiny little sachet bag with a string tied to one end. Buffy sniffed at it.

"Hmmm," she said appreciatively.

"You like it?" Willow asked.

"Smells good. What is it?"

"Just a little something we witches like to call a protection spell," Willow proudly informed her.

"Good deal. Protection," Buffy said, sniffing at the bag again. "I'm surprised, though, 'cause usually spell stuff's more—"

"Stinky." Willow cut her off, nodding. "That's why I added the lavender. Give me time and I may be the first wicca to do all my conjuring in Pine Fresh scent. So what's the plan?"

Buffy frowned and looked at her uncertainly.

"For tonight's slayage," Willow explained. "We're going, aren't we?"

"Oh. Yeah," Buffy replied reluctantly.

"Great!"

"But . . . there's a 'but' here. And it's . . . but you shouldn't come tonight. Is that cool?"

The sadness reached Willow's eyes in an instant, but she made a clear effort to keep it out of her voice. "Sure. Makes sense. You'll be facing big, hairy danger."

"Biggest," Buffy said quickly, not wanting to hurt Willow, but wanting to dissuade her. "And very hairy."

"You're risking your life," Willow continued.

"Right, and why risk yours?" Buffy reasoned.

Willow only looked at her. " 'Cause I'm your friend."

"I know, Will. And that's exactly why I don't want you going. It's too dangerous."

Willow frowned. "But I've done this sort of thing before, like a million times, and I can totally handle myself. Besides . . ." she held up the sachet with the protective spell. "Minty fresh protection. So?"

At the hopeful expression on Willow's face, Buffy hesitated. She felt so awkward, but there was just too much going on in her head right now to bring Willow into what had turned into a volatile situation.

Suddenly, Faith popped her head into the room without a knock.

"Ready? Time to motor. Hey, Willow."

"Hey," Willow replied, barely looking at Faith.

"Uh, look," Buffy ventured. "I really should . . . but we'll hang out later, right?"

"Yeah?" Willow replied, halfheartedly. "You go ahead. I'll just get my stuff."

After a moment's hesitation, Buffy went out with Faith and closed the door behind her.

Back in her room, Willow looked at the sachet and threw it onto the bed. "Stupid," she whispered to herself.

Not long after dark, Giles sat at his desk in his small office in the school library, and struggled to keep from throttling Wesley within an inch of the arrogant pipsqueak's life. The two were engaged in a very polite British argument, but at any moment, Giles thought the time might come when he would have to break Wesley's nose.

"I didn't say you had emotional problems," Wesley went on. "I said you had *an* emotional problem. It's quite different."

Slowly, through gritted teeth, Giles responded. "My attachment to the Slayer is not a problem. In point of fact, it's been a very useful—"

"The way you've handled this assignment is something of an embarrassment to the Council," Wesley informed him.

"If you want to criticize my methods, fine," Giles said, giving up any attempt to hide his disdain for Wesley. "But you can keep your snide remarks to yourself, and while you're at it, don't criticize my methods."

Wesley squared his shoulders and paced. "The fact is, you're no longer qualified to act as Watcher. It's not your fault. You've done well. It's simply time for somebody else to take the field."

Giles stared at him as he paced. Then motion beyond Wesley caught his eye, and he saw them. Just outside the window of his small office, in the main library, four vampires stood glowering in at them.

"Well . . . now's a good time to start."

There were fewer stars in the sky that night, and it seemed darker than usual. Faith liked it that way. Together, she and Buffy strode down a deserted alley in a very nasty section of town, on their way to the warehouse on Devereau that Balthazar had made his lair. They'd been interrupted the night before, but not tonight. Not again. The two Slayers were armed to the teeth. Faith had the compound bow in her hands, and fiddled with it as they walked. Buffy's expression was grim, and she had been unusually silent.

"You're quiet tonight," Faith told her.

Buffy shrugged. "I just want to get this done."

"Yeah, I'm dying to test out the long bow," Faith said excitedly, gazing lovingly at the weapon she had not been willing to give up. "I think it might be my new thing."

"I can't believe you went back for that stuff," Buffy said, raising her eyebrows in amazement.

Faith ignored her. She had started a job, and she was not about to let the cops prevent her from finishing it. As she thought about using the bow on the demon and his lackeys, her stomach rumbled.

"Hey, how do you feel about getting some ribs? You know, after we're done?" she asked.

Buffy opened her mouth to respond . . . and a vampire dropped down from a low roof in the alley to block their way. A second rushed them from behind. With a high kick, Buffy sent the one behind her reeling. The second rushed in at her as Faith struggled to nock an arrow onto the compound bow. She had not practiced with the weapon yet, and couldn't get it together fast enough.

"Screw it," Faith muttered angrily.

The vampire took a swing at her. Faith ducked the blow

and kicked him into the brick wall on the other side of the alley. She gripped the arrow in her hand as though it were a stake, and jabbed it into his heart as he spun around. The leech crumbled to dust.

The two Slayers sprinted down the alley together, trying to get to Balthazar's lair.

"I think we got more coming," Faith said quickly.

"We're never gonna make it to the warehouse," Buffy replied.

"They keep coming one at a time, we got a shot."

Just as she said it, another vampire dropped down into the alley in front of them. Faith slammed him into the wall, then tossed him across the alley to land on some old boxes. Buffy staked him without hesitation, and he was dust.

They moved on, intent upon their goal. As they rounded the corner, a hand reached out from the darkness and gripped Buffy's shoulder. She grabbed the figure in the shadows and threw him, hard, against a Dumpster. He cried out in pain as he hit, then slid down to the filthy pavement.

Faith descended upon him, stake in hand.

"Faith, no!" Buffy screamed.

But it was too late. Faith punched the stake through the man's heart with a sickening crunch.

He did not dust.

He just bled.

Buffy knelt at the man's side as Faith looked on, eyes wide with horror, trying to re-create the preceding moments in her mind. The man touched the blood on his chest and his hands shook. He tried to speak, but could not.

"Don't move . . ." Buffy told him.

"I didn't . . . I didn't know," Faith stammered. She shook her head, denying what her eyes saw; it just was not possible. There was supposed to be only dust, but there was so much blood.

Buffy glanced at her. "We need to call nine-one-one, now!" she shouted.

Faith's mouth opened, but no words came out. She watched helplessly as Buffy turned back to the bleeding man.

"Don't move. It's okay," Buffy whispered as she pushed her hand over the wound, trying to stanch the flow of blood. "I need something to stop the . . ."

Her words trailed off when blood began to drip from the man's mouth. His eyes were wide with shock. As Faith stared at him, the man shuddered and died.

She had killed him; murdered a man in cold blood.

Yet even as the terrible truth of it began to sink in, Faith could feel a sort of numbness beginning to spread through her. She began to retreat to a place inside herself.

That place was very cold and very dark.

CHAPTER 5

Buffy felt as though she were frozen to the spot. The dead man's eyes seemed to stare at her. Blood dripped down his chin and soaked through his shirt. She could not breathe, could not speak, could not move. In that moment, it was as though she herself had died.

Then Faith was tugging at her, pulling her away. "Come on!" Faith urged her. "Come on, we gotta go!"

Buffy was too numb to resist. Faith dragged her away from the cooling corpse and together they ran down the end of the alley. With a hard look, Faith urged her to follow.

"Come on," she said again.

Then she climbed over a low wooden fence at one side of the alley. Buffy watched her go, but could not follow. At the moment, she felt as though she wanted to be as far away as possible from Faith. She looked up to see that on the other side of the alley there was a high chain link fence. Without hesitation, she scaled it and dropped down on the other side.

A moment later she was out on the street. Cars drove by and she slipped between them and hurried to a tunnel just on the other side. A dark figure appeared in her peripheral vision. Heart pounding, Buffy turned, and was startled to find Angel standing before her.

"Angel," she stammered weakly.

"Buffy. I've been looking for you."

Her heart beat faster. She wanted to tell him, wanted him to take her in his arms and tell her it would be all right. But she could not put it into words just yet. That would make it all too real.

Suddenly he frowned, sniffed the air. Then he grabbed her wrist and pulled her arm toward him. He had scented the blood there and now he stared at it. Then she pulled it away quickly.

"Your hand," he said, concern etched in his face.

"It's okay," she said softly.

He blinked, but did not question her. "I've just been to the warehouse. I was waiting for you. They've got Giles."

Buffy shivered. It had seemed unreal before, and she had thought it could not get worse. But suddenly it had.

Faith lurked in the darkened alley and watched as the police car slid by like a shark patrolling its territory. She had not gotten far before she had felt the pull of the dead man at her. Eventually, she had backtracked and now she found herself there again, standing over him, studying his dull, lifeless eyes, and the drying blood on the front of his shirt.

Something had died inside her, as well.

Where her blood had surged with wild life and blazed with heat, it now ran cold.

Drawn by some lure she could not comprehend, she knelt by the body. It looked almost unreal, like a mannequin made up to look like a corpse. Barely able to breathe, she reached out and touched her fingers to the bloody wound at his chest.

It was not a mannequin.

The dead man was real.

She had killed him.

In Balthazar's warehouse lair, Giles and Wesley stood side by side, hands tied behind their backs, flanked by members of the Eliminati. With dawning horror and utter revulsion, they watched as the disgusting, blubbery demon was bathed in ladled water by his vampire slaves.

"The front, the front," Balthazar gurgled wetly. "Moisten the front."

"Oh, God," Wesley whispered to himself. "Oh, God."

"Doesn't seem too promising, does it?" Giles remarked quietly.

"Stay calm, Mr. Giles, we have to stay calm," Wesley rasped.

"Well, thank God you're here," Giles replied dryly. "I was planning to panic."

"What is that thing?" Wesley whispered, appalled.

"That would be your demon. You know, the dead one?"

"There's no need to get snippy."

Balthazar moaned in relief as the water washed over him. His blazing eyes settled on the Watchers. "Bring them closer."

The vampires grabbed Giles and Wesley brutally and trundled them up right in front of the demon's bathing tank.

"You know what I want," Balthazar spat.

"If it's for me to scrub those hard to reach areas," Giles said coolly, "I'd like to request you kill me now."

One of the Eliminati rabbit-punched him from behind. Giles grunted in pain. "Ow," the Watcher replied.

"Are you out of your mind?" Wesley whimpered. "This is hardly the time for games."

"Why not? They're going to torture us to death anyway."

Balthazar chuckled. "He's not wrong about that."

"Now hold on!" Wesley protested. "We have something you want, you have something we want."

The demon considered. "Mmm, a trade, intriguing." It frowned. "No, wait, boring. Pull off his kneecaps!"

The vampires rushed him, and Wesley screamed. "No! The Slayer gave it to someone. A tall man, a friend of hers. I can tell you everything."

"Quiet, you twerp," Giles snarled at him. "They'll kill us both."

"But . . . I like to have . . . kneecaps," Wesley stammered.

"You *will* tell us everything!" the demon roared.

Wesley shuddered. "Yes, sir . . ."

"What is this friend's name?" Balthazar demanded.

Defeated, Wesley lowered his head. "I . . . didn't actually catch it."

"Tell you what," Giles sighed. "Let Captain Courageous here go and I'll tell you what you want to know. How's that deal?"

Water sloshed in the tank as Balthazar shook with rage and screamed at them. "There is one deal! You will die quickly or you will die slowly! The man who has my amulet, what is his name?"

"His name is Angel."

Giles blinked at the voice and turned to see Angel—in full vamp-face—stride confidently into the room and launch himself at the Eliminati. He tore into them with a vigor and cruelty that surprised even Giles.

Not that the Watcher had any problem with that, given that Angel was in the process of saving his life.

One of the vampires rushed at the two men, and Giles gave him a solid head-butt that put him down hard. When he glanced up, skull smarting from that move, he saw Buffy drop down into the warehouse from atop a pile of large shipping crates. The Eliminati rushed her, and she fought them off handily.

He knew his Slayer.

Buffy beat the vampire closest to her and relieved him of his sword. Expecting her next move, Giles turned his back to her, exposing his tied wrists. Buffy brought the sword around and down with one swift, precise move, and slashed the ropes away.

The warehouse was filled with the sound of swords clanging as they missed their marks, and fists striking flesh as Buffy and Angel battered the Eliminati mercilessly.

"Unacceptable!" Balthazar screeched, gasping for air. "Unacceptable!"

Giles worked Wesley free of his restraints just as a vampire swordsman approached from behind him. He shoved Wesley out of the way and ducked the blade as it whistled through the air. The sword clanged off the wall and Giles stood up tall and grabbed the swordsman's wrist. He slammed his elbow back and shattered the Eliminati's nose, then tore the sword from his grasp.

Another vampire swordsman approached. He swung his blade, and Giles parried. A second attack and Giles knocked the blade away and rammed his fist into the vampire's face.

When he looked up, Wesley was a prisoner again. One of Balthazar's vampiric henchmen had grabbed him in a tight hold from behind.

"Mr. Giles!" Wesley cried, panicked.

The blood surged through Giles's heart. He had not felt this invigorated in a very long time. He brought the blade up and swung it with all his might toward Wesley's neck.

"Down!" he roared.

Wesley tucked his head down as best he could. It was just enough. The blade severed the vampire's head neatly from its shoulders, and the thing showered cinder and ash down upon the crouching Wesley.

There were many Eliminati, but they were no match for Buffy and Angel. The Slayer and her one-time love, the vampire with a soul, battered and broke the demon's sword-wielding slugs, barely taking a hit themselves. Giles glanced over in alarm to see that Balthazar had realized it too—El Eliminati were losing.

The demon roared and reached out toward Angel. Waves of power emanated from him, and Angel was lifted off his feet and yanked toward the bathing tank as if by a magnet. Balthazar grabbed Angel by the head and began to crush his skull. Angel grunted in pain and tried to fight him off, but to no avail.

Giles started toward Angel, but even as he did he glanced over at Buffy to see that her gaze was not on Angel and the demon, but on a heavy, industrial light hanging from a bare cable above the tank. He smiled thinly as he realized what she was about to do.

With a single pull, Buffy tore the cable from its moorings on the ceiling and the lamp plummeted down into Balthazar's bathing tank. The demon screeched in pain and shuddered as the electricity running through the water thoroughly cooked it.

The stench was awful.

Angel fell to the ground beside the tank. Buffy went to him and helped him up. Even as she did, Balthazar's eyes popped open and he wheezed painfully.

"Slayer . . . you think you've won?" the demon rasped, and chuckled weakly. "When he rises . . . you'll wish . . . I'd killed you all."

Balthazar looked as though he might say more. Then a final, fetid breath was pumped from his lungs, his eyes closed, and the demon was well and truly dead.

Very late that night, long after even the cleaning crew had gone home, the Mayor knelt within a pentagram he had drawn in the rotunda of City Hall. Five white candles burned at each point of the star. Across the rotunda, Mr.

Trick stood beside the cage in which Vincent of the Eliminati squatted, glowering. The Mayor held his arms out and chanted fluently in Latin. The words were familiar enough to him that he did not even have to translate them in his mind. He spoke them in Latin, but heard them in his head in English.

"I call upon the forces of our mother in darkness, protect your unholy son from harm . . . now . . . and forever!"

All of City Hall shook from the foundations, a shower of loosened dust sifting down to the floor. After several moments, the tremor passed.

The Mayor glanced at his watch, a bit disappointed. "I don't understand why Allan would miss this. He's usually so punctual."

He stood and brushed off his pants, then looked up to find Trick staring at him.

"Did it work?"

"Let's find out. Open the cage," the Mayor replied nonchalantly.

"You sure?" Trick asked dubiously.

"Oh, hold on," the Mayor said. He did a little tiptoe across the room, grabbed Vincent's sword, then slipped it into the cage to the vampire. Then he stepped back and regarded the cage again. "Okay, now we're ready."

Shaking his head, Trick sauntered over and unlocked the cage. With a roar of fury, Vincent rushed from the cage and brought the sword down, cleaving the Mayor's head in two, down to the neck.

The halves of the Mayor's head dangled to either side for a moment. He was amazed to find that he could still see.

The expression on Vincent's face was priceless.

After a moment, the two halves of the Mayor's head reconnected, the flesh healing as though nothing at all had happened to him. His vampire attacker staggered back, staring at him in shock.

Trick staked him through the back and Vincent exploded into dust.

The Mayor reached into his jacket pocket and removed his "To Do" list for the day. Right between "call Temp agency" and "Meeting with PTA" was "become invincible." He pulled out a pencil and put a check right next to it.

"Well," he said casually, "this officially commences the hundred days. Nothing can harm me until the Ascension." He began to giggle like a small boy. "Gosh, I'm feeling chipper. Who's for a root beer?"

In the bathroom in her motel room, Faith scrubbed hard to get the blood out of her clothes from the night before. The sunlight seemed grimy through the windows. A bit of red swirled in the water in the sink.

There was a knock at the door and Faith glanced up, heart skipping a beat.

"Faith. It's me." *Buffy's voice.*

Slowly, a bit reluctantly, she crossed the room and opened the door. Buffy was dressed conservatively, almost as though she had just come from church.

"Hey," she said.

Faith did not meet her eyes. "Hey." She walked back across the room and into the bathroom to continue scrubbing. Buffy closed the door, then followed her. In the doorway, she watched Faith for a few seconds.

"So, how you doing?" she asked.

"I'm all right," Faith said, revealing nothing. "You know me."

"Faith, we need to talk about what we're going to do."

"There's nothing to talk about," she snapped, and threw a quick, angry glance at Buffy. "I was doing my job."

Buffy stared at her. "Being a Slayer is not the same as being a killer. Faith, please don't shut me out here. Sooner or later we're both gonna have to deal."

Faith ignored her, wringing out her shirt. "Wrong."

"We can help each other."

"I don't need it," Faith said. She pulled the stopper out of the sink and walked out into the room, carrying her wet clothes.

"Yeah?" Buffy replied. "Who's wrong now? Faith, you can shut off all the emotions that you want, but eventually they're gonna find a body."

Faith spun and glared at her. "Okay, this is the last time we're having this conversation and we're not even having it now, you understand me? There is no body. I took it, weighted it, and dumped it. The body doesn't exist."

Buffy stared at her in shock. Faith felt the brunt of that look, but she pushed it away, just as she had buried all the emotions that had come upon her the night before, when her life had become a nightmare.

Now she had woken from that nightmare, and she was not about to allow Buffy to start it up again.

"Getting rid of the evidence doesn't make the problem go away," Buffy argued.

"It does for me," Faith replied lightly.

"Faith, you don't get it! You killed a man."

"No, *you* don't get it." Faith smiled at her. "I. Don't. Care."

Lost

Faith could not sleep. After Buffy had left the motel she had tried, but images of the dead man's face swam up at her whenever she closed her eyes. Eventually she had risen, dressed, and gone out walking again.

She did not wander this time. She knew exactly where she wanted to go.

Now she stood at a railing and stared out at the water. Somewhere down there, weighted to keep him down, was a corpse with wide, frightened eyes and a hole right through his heart. She watched the moonlight flicker in the ripples on the surface of the water and thought about the dead man, but she felt nothing, would not allow herself to feel anything at all.

That was good. It was better that way. Less complicated.

Faith was hollow, now. She was empty inside.

Lost

CONSEQUENCES

CONSEQUENCES

dumped his body in the ocean, and now

Chapter 1

*D*rowning.

Salt water burned her throat and eyes as Buffy thrashed against the currents of the ocean that swirled around her. Shafts of sunlight sliced down from above. She was so close to the surface that she could taste the sweet air . . . but instead she choked down more sea water.

The current . . .

But it wasn't the current. Something had hold of her leg. Its grip was like an iron shackle, a chain, an anchor dragging her farther into the depths, away from the sweet glimpse of sun from above. Blackness began to seep into Buffy's vision and she knew at any second she would lose consciousness. She was going to die. If only she could be free of the anchor that weighted her down.

Desperate, she glanced beneath her.

The iron clasp around her ankle was a hand. The hand of a dead man, eyes wide. Faith had killed him and dumped his body in the ocean, and now he was punishing

*Buffy for her part in it. Her corpse would also drift with
the tides.*

*More salt water filled her lungs and stomach and she
retched. With the tiny bit of strength she held in reserve,
she kicked out, away from him, shook herself loose of his
rigid grip—a rigor mortis grip—and pulled herself up toward the sun.*

*Buffy broke the surface and gasped for air. Motion
above caught her eye. She glanced up and saw Faith
above her. Faith's hands were on Buffy, but her eyes were
cold. As dead as the waterlogged corpse below.*

*Faith shoved her under again and held her there. Buffy
kicked and fought and began to drown . . .*

Her eyes snapped open and for the first few seconds,
Buffy did nothing but breathe. It had been a dream, true,
but all too real to her. It was as though she had actually
been deprived of air.

After a moment, she sat up in bed, groggy, and wiped
the sleep from her eyes. Despair lingered from her dream
as she roused herself from bed, and dragged her feet
crossing the room. Down the hall, she could hear voices
on the television in her mother's room.

". . . breaking news about the murder that shocked the
Mayor and residents of Sunnydale," said a male voice.

Buffy stepped in behind her mother, who sat in a chair
in front of the TV, one leg drawn up beneath her. On the
screen, a fishing boat hauled something unidentifiable out
of the water.

The voice that broke in then was female, that of the reporter on the scene. "Fishermen discovered the body
today, the victim of a brutal stabbing. Authorities and cit-
izens alike were shocked when the slain man was identified as Deputy Mayor Allan Finch."

The dream, Buffy thought immediately. Like many she

had had since she had become the Slayer, it had been an echo of reality. She had not recognized Finch when Faith had killed him, but his face had seemed vaguely familiar. Now she knew why.

Faith had vowed they would never find a body.

But she had been wrong.

Buffy stared at the television and nausea roiled in her stomach. Bile rose in her throat, and it had the faintest taste of sea water.

"Still reeling from the news," the reporter said, "Mayor Wilkins had this to say. . . ."

The screen cut from the reporter to a press conference at City Hall. The Mayor looked saddened indeed, as he addressed the media.

"Mr. Finch was not only my longtime aide and associate," the Mayor noted, "he was a close, personal friend. I promise you I will not rest until whoever did this is found and brought to justice."

Suddenly, Joyce Summers sensed her daughter standing behind her, and turned to cast a troubled look at Buffy.

"Oh, honey, you're up," Joyce said. "It's just terrible, isn't it?"

Buffy felt like the world was closing in all around her.

Though she dragged her feet all morning, that numb, sick feeling staying with her all along, Buffy managed to make it to school in time. During her free period, she went to the library to see Giles and, reluctantly, to report to Wesley. The place had not seemed the same to her since Wesley came. It was still Giles's domain, certainly, but some of what made the library *their* place had been taken away.

And now, well, *nothing* seemed the same.

When she pushed through the library doors, Buffy felt herself flinch. Faith was already there. She glanced at Buffy for only a second and then looked away, but she gave no indication that anything at all was wrong. Buffy wanted to scream at her, at all of them. It was like the whole world had been turned inside out, and nobody had noticed.

Most of all, though, she wanted Faith to talk to her. Though the other Slayer was silent, Buffy could tell just by looking at her that something dark and dangerous was building inside Faith. The way she held her body, the way she moved, as though at any moment she might come under attack, it was obvious that Faith was still in shock, never mind in denial.

Total denial, Buffy thought.

But there was nothing she could do about it in front of Giles and Wesley. She owed Faith that much, at least, to keep it to herself until they had had more of a chance to talk.

Wesley asked Buffy to take a seat and began to pace. It was only then that she noticed how troubled he and Giles both seemed. Then he explained what was bothering him, and Buffy's heart skipped a beat. Her throat became dry. Wesley had heard about the murder of Allan Finch, and it had somehow, inexplicably, turned into a tiny personal crusade for him.

This will never go away, Buffy thought dismally. She tried to catch Faith's eye again, but the girl would just not look at her.

Wesley paused in his pacing for just a moment, glanced at the two Slayers, and then resumed. "I want you to look into this. Find out everything you can about the murder of the Deputy Mayor."

Buffy cringed inwardly. "But that's . . . I mean, it's not really our jurisdiction. Is it?"

"It's no big, B," Faith said coolly. "We'll get into it if he wants."

Horrified, but unable to let her feelings show, Buffy

could only turn and stare at Faith. *How can she be so . . . casual about this?*

"No, Buffy's right," Giles intoned. "The Deputy Mayor's murder was the result of human malice. There's nothing supernatural about it."

Wesley frowned. He seemed to puff up a bit, as though trying to take up even more of the space around him, the space that had for so long belonged to Giles. "We don't know that for certain. I believe it merits investigation."

"Which I'm sure the police are doing," Giles replied tiredly. "Meantime, if you ask me, there are better uses for the Slayers' time."

"Ah, but I don't believe I did," Wesley noted pointedly. "Ask you."

"Considering the success of your previous adventure—"

Giles might have gone on, but at that moment, Cordelia strutted into the library. As always, she seemed out of place in the room, a creature of image in a room filled with thoughts on paper, dusty old tomes and textbooks she would never even glance at by choice.

"Don't let me interrupt," Cordelia said, then shook her head. "Wait, let me interrupt. I'm in a hurry."

None of them could have missed the slack-jawed gaze of admiration Wesley gave her. He was smitten on sight.

"What did you need?" Giles asked.

"Psych class," Cordelia explained. "Freud and Jung. Book me."

"Happily," Giles replied.

As Giles walked off into the stacks to fetch the books, obviously relieved to be away from his replacement, Cordy turned to regard Wesley. She glanced him over, though with nowhere near the awe he had attached to the process when he'd done the same to her a moment ago.

She did smile the tiniest bit, however. "Check out Giles, the next generation. What's your deal?"

Wesley could not find his tongue. He mumbled a few incoherent words before Faith interrupted.

"New Watcher."

The whole scene seemed surreal to Buffy. Faith was the calm and collected one, the reliable one all of a sudden. Even to the point where she was providing the explanations. Giles seemed almost as lost as Buffy felt. Nothing was right. Everything was falling apart, and this place, which had once felt like a second home to her, now seemed somehow foreign.

Cordelia raised an eyebrow at Faith's words. "Oh."

Wesley turned to cast a disapproving glance at Buffy. "Does everybody know about you?"

"She's a friend," Buffy replied dully, just wanting Cordelia to leave. Wanting to leave herself.

"Let's not exaggerate." Cordelia looked Wesley over again. The second time seemed a bit more acceptable than the first. "So you're the new Watcher?" she asked, obvious flirtation in her voice.

"Wesley Wyndam-Pryce."

He offered his hand and she took it, held it for a moment.

"I like a man with two last names," she said. "I'm Cordelia."

"And you teach psychology?" Wesley asked, obviously enchanted.

"I *take* psychology," she replied.

Giles appeared with the books Cordelia needed and passed behind Wesley. "She's a student."

Wesley pulled his hand back quickly, as though he'd been stung. "Oh, w-w-well, I uh, yes," he stammered. "In fact I am. Here to watch. Girls. Uh, Buffy and Faith, to be specific."

Cordelia's eyes lit up. "Well, it's about time we got some fresh blood around here."

"Well," Wesley chuckled self-consciously. "Fresh. Yes."

At the book checkout counter, Giles was stamping the texts for Cordelia. "Here you go."

"Thanks," Cordelia said. Then she turned back to Wesley and beamed. "Welcome to Sunnydale."

Wesley stared after her as she sauntered out. "My, she's . . . cheeky."

"Uh, first word 'jail,' second word 'bait,' " Faith chimed in.

The young Watcher cleared his throat and turned to them. "Well. Where were we?"

Despite the amusement of it all, Buffy felt not even the slightest hint of humor. Her face was slack, her entire body cold. "Done," she said quickly, tense. "I mean, we *were* done, right?"

Faith stood up quickly. "Yep. Off to patrol, so we'll see you."

"One moment, girls," Wesley said abruptly. "I'm your commander, now. And on the matter of this murder, I am resolved. Natural or *super,* I want to know."

Buffy swallowed hard.

"Fine by me," Faith offered. "Always ready to kick a little bad guy butt."

They were side by side as they left the library, but Faith was so cold, so distant, that Buffy had never felt the differences between them more keenly. Without a word, as if communicating by some psychic connection, they moved down the hall to the first empty room they found, an English classroom. Once inside, Buffy closed the door, glancing around with mounting paranoia.

"So, you gonna rat me out?" Faith asked, almost nonchalantly. "Is that it?"

It all come boiling up out of Buffy in an instant. She could not take holding it in even a second more. "Faith, we have to tell. I can't pretend to investigate this. I can't pretend that I don't know."

"Oh, I see, but you can pretend that Angel's still dead when you need to protect *him*."

"I am trying to protect you," Buffy argued. "Look, if we don't do the right thing, it's only gonna make things worse for you."

Faith frowned deeply. "Worse than jail for the rest of my young life? No way."

Buffy shook her head. "Faith, what we did——"

"Yeah. We. You were right there beside me when this whole thing went down. Anything I have to answer for, you do, too. You're a part of this, B, all the way."

With that, Faith stormed out of the room and slammed the door behind her. At first, Buffy was paralyzed. She had no idea how to go on, how to even go about her day, knowing what she knew. If she spoke up, Faith would never forgive her, but if she kept silent, she would never forgive *herself*.

Feeling lost, she rose and left the classroom. Down the hall, she saw Willow sitting on a sofa in the lounge, reading. Buffy's heart sparked just a little. She needed someone to talk to, and no one knew her like Willow did.

"Hey," Buffy said as she sat down beside her.

"Hey," Willow replied, a bit hesitantly. "Where's Faith? I saw her around. Figure you two were gonna go kill some more nasty stuff."

"Not right now," Buffy told her, hands folded nervously in her lap. "I think she bailed."

An awkward moment passed. Then Buffy turned to her and began to talk, to open up. Just as Willow spoke as well. They both stopped and looked away.

"Um, you go ahead," Buffy said.

"I'm . . . late," Willow said. She began to gather her things and shove them into her backpack. "I'm meeting Michael. The warlock guy? We're still trying to de-rat Amy."

Sadly, Buffy nodded. "Okay," she said softly.

Willow rose and went off without looking back. "So, see ya."

"See ya," Buffy replied.

But Willow was already gone. Buffy was alone again.

Darkness fell swiftly across Sunnydale, as though anxious for the creatures of the night to be out and about their business. Angel was more than willing to oblige. The vampire clung to the shadows as he leaned against a brick wall at the end of the alley where he had run into Buffy several nights earlier.

A pair of police cars were parked nearby, their blue lights spinning, throwing ghosts upon the walls. In the alley, policemen and crime scene staffers collected evidence. A detective spoke to a local woman.

"So you heard the man scream about what time last night?"

"I'm not sure," the woman replied. "Seven, maybe eight?"

"Can you be more specific?" the detective prodded. "Maybe between seven and seven-thirty?"

Angel narrowed his eyes, deeply troubled. He watched a crime scene guy scraping dried blood from the front of a metal Dumpster. His mind flashed immediately to the night before, and the blood he saw smeared all over Buffy's hand. She had said it was nothing, and he had been more concerned with Balthazar at the time. As long as she was not wounded, he figured it was no cause for concern.

Haunted by the memory, Angel turned and strode quickly away from the site.

The Mayor stood in his office, glumly slipping one document after another through the paper shredder. The machine seemed almost to drag the paper hungrily from his grasp.

Mr. Trick entered the office with a file folder in his hand.

"It's not working," the Mayor told him, shaking his head grumpily.

"It's supposed to do something besides shred?" Trick inquired.

"It's supposed to cheer me up!" The Mayor said, a bit snippy. "Usually using the shredder gives me a lift. It's fun."

Trick paused for a moment. "And today you're not getting the ya-yas."

"No," the Mayor said huffily. "Guess it'll take more than this to turn my frown upside down. I just don't understand why Allan would leave such a paper trail about our dealings."

The thought gave him pause. He ran another page through and looked up at Trick. "Do you think he was going to betray me? Oh, now that's a horrible thought. And now he's dead and I'll never have the chance to scold him."

"Maybe this will change your mood," Trick said. He tossed the file onto the Mayor's desk.

"What is it?" The Mayor picked up the file and opened it.

"Bombshell," Trick said simply.

Eyes wide, the Mayor read with interest.

"The Deputy Mayor had wooden splinters in his wound," Trick summarized. "Struck right through the heart with a sharp, pointed object. Now, word is someone was fighting vampires not a block away from the scene. Smart money says it's a Slayer did this job."

Startled, the Mayor regarded him carefully. "What, you think he talked? To them?"

Trick grinned. "If he did, I'm thinking he said the wrong thing."

The Mayor smiled, feeling more than a tad peppier. He closed the file. "Well. This *is* exciting. A Slayer up for Murder One. That's sunshine and roses to me. It really is."

CHAPTER 2

Morbid. *Perverse.* Those were the two words that kept running around Buffy's head as she and Faith broke into City Hall, and then into the Deputy Mayor's office upstairs. Their pretense to be investigating was a bizarre kind of masquerade, one that made Buffy feel ill, and yet it was as though she were simply being carried along by these events. As though it were her inarguable fate, no less her destiny than being the Slayer.

That was crap. She knew it. But it was all that was keeping her functioning while her mind gnawed at her dilemma over and over again.

In darkness, they slipped into the Deputy Mayor's office. Once the door was closed, Faith turned on the light. The office itself was completely unremarkable, boring and staid.

"I'm telling you, we did the world a favor," Faith said as she glanced around. "This guy was about as interesting as watching paint dry."

"Faith," Buffy chided.

"Joking," Faith replied. "Jeez, lighten up a little, B."

But even as she spoke, Faith spotted a framed photo on Finch's desk. She picked it up and studied it for a moment. Over her shoulder, Buffy could see that it was a picture of Finch himself and the Mayor. The dead man was smiling sweetly.

"He came out of nowhere," Faith said, voice heavy with what Buffy hoped was regret.

Buffy was relieved to hear the pain in the other Slayer's voice. It meant there was hope.

"I know," she said with sympathy.

At that, though, Faith's eyes went cold again. "Whatever," she said, the word almost a sneer. She put the photo back on the man's desk. "I'm not looking to hug and cry and learn and grow, I'm just saying it happened quick, y'know?"

Buffy flinched. After a moment, the two of them went back to searching the Deputy Mayor's office. But only seconds later, Faith slammed his desk drawer, frustrated.

"You know what? Let's just blow," she said. "Who cares what this guy was about? It's kinda moot now, don't you think?"

But Buffy had been thinking about Finch a lot, and she was not ready to give up so easily. "I don't think he was in that alley by chance. I think he was looking for us. Like to know why."

"So, what, you think there's some big conspiracy?" Faith scoffed.

Buffy pulled open a file cabinet drawer. Every single file was completely empty. She turned to Faith. "You were saying?"

"So his papers are gone. That doesn't prove anything."

Buffy regarded her coolly. "Except that somebody doesn't want us to prove anything."

It was troubling, but there was nothing more for them to find in Finch's office. Silently, they moved to the door.

Buffy opened it and glanced into the hallway. They had just begun to slip out when a door was opened a short way down the corridor. The Mayor stepped out with another man in tow. Buffy stared in astonishment. The guy with the Mayor—she had seen him before.

He was a vampire.

"Get as many men on it as you can," the Mayor told the vamp.

Buffy closed the door and she and Faith leaned against it. Even through it, they could hear the vampire's response.

"Yeah. We'll be wanting to turn up the heat."

Nothing after that. The Mayor and his friend had walked away. Buffy counted silently to one hundred, and then she and Faith left City Hall as quickly as possible. They were silent until they had put a few blocks between themselves and the site of their breaking-and-entering. They strolled together downtown as though the world had not been irrevocably altered in the previous twenty-four hours.

"So the Mayor of Sunnydale is a black hat. That's a shocker, huh?" Faith drawled.

"Actually, yeah," Buffy replied. "I didn't get the bad guy vibe off him."

Faith shook her head in amusement. "When you gonna learn, B? It doesn't matter what kind of vibe you get off a person, 'cause nine times out of ten, the face they're showing you is not the real one."

Grim-faced, Buffy froze on the sidewalk and eyed Faith warily. "I guess you'd know a lot about that."

Slowly, eyes narrowed, Faith turned and glared at her. "What is that supposed to mean?"

"It's just . . . look at you, Faith. Less than twenty-four hours ago, you killed a man. And now it's all zipidee-doo-dah? That's not your real face, and I know it. I know what you're feeling because I'm feeling it, too."

"Do you?" Faith asked, tilting her head to one side. "So fill me in, 'cause I'd like to hear this."

"Dirty." Buffy kept her eyes locked on Faith's. "Like something sick creeped inside you and you can't get it out. And you keep hoping it was some nightmare, but it wasn't. And we are gonna have to figure out—"

"Is there gonna be an intermission in this?" Faith asked, feigning boredom.

At least Buffy hoped it was feigned.

"Just let me talk to Giles, okay? I swear—"

"No," Faith snapped. "We're not bringing anybody else into this. You gotta keep your head, B. This is all going to blow over in a few days."

"And if it doesn't?"

Faith shrugged. "If it doesn't? They got a freighter leaving the docks at least twice a day. It ain't fancy, but it gets you gone."

"And then what?" Buffy asked, nerves frayed. "You just leave with it? You see the dead guy in your head every day for the rest of your life?"

"Buffy, I'm not going to *see* anything," Faith countered. She took a step closer, watching Buffy's eyes. "I missed the mark last night, and I'm sorry about the guy, I really am. But it happens. Anyways, how many people do you think we've saved by now? Thousands? And didn't you stop the world from ending? Because in *my* book, that puts you and me in the plus column."

Angry now, Buffy shook her head. "We help people! That doesn't mean we can do whatever we want!"

"Why not?" Faith scoffed. "This guy I offed was no Gandhi. I mean, we just saw he was mixed up in dirty dealings."

"Maybe," Buffy snapped, almost nose to nose with Faith now. "But what if he was coming to us for help?"

"What if he was? You're still not seeing the big picture,

B. Something made us different. We're warriors. We were built to kill—"

"To kill demons! But it does not mean that we get to pass judgment on people like we're better than everyone else!"

"We *are* better," Faith said simply. "That's right. Better. People need us to survive. In the balance? Nobody's gonna cry over some random bystander who got caught in the crossfire."

Stricken, Buffy could only gape at her. At length, she swallowed hard.

"I am."

Faith just shook her head. "That's your loss."

She walked away, leaving Buffy to stare after her in horror. The entire walk back to her house, she played the scene, the confrontation, over and over in her mind. She had no idea how to proceed. Buffy knew that she had to tell Giles, had to come clean, for her own sake, and for Faith's. The girl needed help whether she wanted it or not. But some part of her fought against the idea of revealing Faith's secret, branded it disloyal.

Buffy had to let the truth out, but one way or another, she knew it was going to hurt.

The burden of her guilt and the secret hanging heavy over her, she walked up to her front door. Before she could even pull out her keys, her mother opened the door from inside, a look of panic on her face.

"Buffy . . ." Joyce began.

Behind her, Buffy could see a balding man with a mustache. His face was familiar. It only took her a moment to realize it was Detective Stein, a policeman she had met before.

Her breath caught in her throat.

Inside, she sat across from her mother in the living room as Detective Stein questioned her.

"Tell me again. You got home at what time last night?"

"Late," Buffy admitted. "A little past one, I guess."

Detective Stein frowned. "Maybe you can explain to me what a girl your age is doing out all night."

"We were at Faith's. Watching TV."

"What did you watch?"

"Infomercial," she said flatly. "Is that it? I'm . . . I'm kind of beat."

"Yeah, I have enough for now," Stein replied. "Buffy, if you know something, if you're protecting someone . . ."

She took a short, shallow breath. "I wish I could help you."

In her motel room, Faith scowled at Detective Stein. *Moron,* she thought, wanting to know what she'd been doing out all night. Here she was, obviously on her own, living in a motel room. She could do whatever the hell she wanted.

"Just hangin'," she lied.

"Hanging," he repeated doubtfully. "By yourself?"

"No. I was with my friend Buffy. Watching some old movie."

"That's funny," Stein said slowly. " 'Cause I've got a couple witnesses who put you near the alley."

Faith shook her head. "Witnesses?"

The detective paced the floor a bit. Then he turned his intense gaze upon her again. "Somebody stabbed this guy through the heart. Strange thing is, the weapon? It was made out of wood. Any of this mean anything to you?"

"Yeah. That whoever did it wasn't hip to the Bronze Age."

Stein frowned, moved a step closer, trying to intimidate her. "I promise you, it'd be better for everyone if you'd just come clean."

"You mean am I covering for someone? Hardly. I'm

not the 'throw myself on the sword' type," Faith informed him bluntly.

The cop sighed, then nodded. "Well, call me if you remember anything."

He handed Faith his card, and walked out. She stared at the door for a long time after he'd gone.

Angel had been watching Faith's room all night. When the Detective came out, he watched the man climb into his car and drive off. Brow furrowed with concern, he watched Faith's door, and waited, not liking the thoughts that filled his head.

Not liking them at all.

Willow sat in her bedroom working at her computer, surrounded by all the things that usually made her happy. At the moment, they weren't working. For days, she had been feeling more than a little abandoned by her best friend, and yet she could not help but feel guilty at the way she took off on Buffy earlier in the day. It was not the only thing on her mind—boyfriend and homework made sure of that—but it lingered in her head like a ghost.

When somebody rapped on the French doors that led from her room out to the backyard, Willow glanced over and was both anxious and relieved to see that it was Buffy.

"Hey," Buffy said, as Willow let her in.

"Hey."

"I need to talk to you."

Willow nodded. "Good. 'Cause I've been letting things fester, and I don't like it. I want to be fester-free."

"Yeah," Buffy agreed, closing the doors behind her. "Me too."

"I mean, don't get me wrong," Willow said in an awkward rush, wanting to get it all out now that she'd begun. "I completely understand why you and Faith have been doing the bonding thing. You guys work together. You should get along."

"It's more complicated than that," Buffy replied, eyes downcast.

Willow bristled. "But see, it's that exact thing that's ticking me off. It's this whole 'Slayers only' attitude. Since when wouldn't I understand? You talk to me about everything. It's like, all of a sudden I'm not cool enough for you because I can't kill things with my bare hands."

Almost before Willow had gotten the words out, Buffy's eyes went wide with pain and despair, and she clapped a hand to her mouth to cover her sob as she burst into tears.

"Oh," Willow said, stunned, "oh, Buffy, don't cry." She took her friend in her arms and Buffy hugged her close. "I'm sorry. I was too hard on you. Sometimes I unleash, and I don't know my own strength."

She pulled back and looked at the Slayer, but Buffy was still weeping. Willow did not understand. Buffy almost never broke down this way. It was as though she had been shattered from the inside.

"It's bad," Willow went on, trying to find new ways to apologize. "I'm bad. I'm a bad, bad, bad person."

Buffy stared at her, but only for a moment. "Will," she said, "I'm in trouble."

Then she began to talk. Willow sat down on the bed beside her, in this place that was her haven, where she was always supposed to feel safe and secure and comforted. Then Buffy told her a story that shocked and saddened her, and left her with a hollow feeling in her stomach, and Willow did not feel safe at all.

". . . and Faith just acts like she doesn't care," Buffy finished. "The way she talks it's like she didn't even make a mistake."

"Do you think she's, like, in shock?" Willow suggested, though it sounded empty, even to her.

"I don't know. But I think that detective knows more than he's saying. I think he knew that I was lying."

"You have to go to Giles, Buffy," Willow said softly. "He'll know what to do."

The lights were on in the library when Buffy walked in, but the place was silent as a tomb. Usually there was a kind of life to it, an energy, particularly when they were all together, planning something. But tonight it was cold and sterile, and at first, she thought no one was there.

"Giles?" she called out.

At the sound of her voice, he emerged from his inner office, walking slowly, a contemplative expression on his face. He was dressed well, as always, and yet he seemed rumpled, his face and clothes both made her wonder what he had been through. The last thing she wanted was to give him another burden, but she could not carry it on her own. She needed him.

"Buffy," he said, softly. He looked at her expectantly.

"Um, I don't really know how to say this," she began. Then she steeled herself. Took a breath. "So, I'm . . . I'm just gonna say it. I know I've kept things from you before, but—"

Someone moved back in Giles's office. Buffy glanced over and saw Faith come out behind him. The other Slayer just looked at her. Waiting. Her heart skipped a beat and a sense of defeat, an urge to surrender, swept through her.

"But . . ." Buffy muttered, her words trailing off. She stared at Faith, torn once more about how to proceed. "I've been blowing off my classes. You know, in the sense of not attending—"

"It's okay, Buffy," Faith interrupted. "I told him."

Buffy gaped at her. "You told him?"

"I had to," Faith said innocently. "He had to know what you did."

"What I did?" Buffy asked, mystified.

Only when Faith would not meet her gaze did Buffy allow herself to realize what the other girl had done. It was so devious, so cunning, so heartless, that only then did Buffy truly begin to see the scope of Faith's retreat into darkness and denial.

"Giles, no," Buffy said, voice barely above a whisper. "That's not what happened."

"I don't want to hear it, Buffy," the Watcher said gravely. "I don't want to hear any more lies."

Buffy glared at Faith, feeling her betrayal deeply. "You can't be serious. You're setting me up?"

Still, Faith would not look at her. Buffy's mind whirled, trying to come to terms both with Faith's cunning and with Giles's harsh tone. *How could she do it? How could he believe it, even for a minute?*

"Get in my office now," Giles barked at her. "Faith, I'll talk to you in the morning."

"Giles, please," Buffy begged. "You have to—"

"Now!" he snapped.

Buffy stared at him for a moment, then walked, defeated, into his office. She made no further attempt at eye contact with Faith. Inside, she heard Faith leaving. A moment later, Giles walked in, his face ashen.

"Giles, I swear, I didn't do this," Buffy said quickly, trying to reason with him. "Look, I know I messed up badly, but the murder, it was—"

"Faith," he finished for her. "I know."

Her mouth dropped open.

"She may have many talents, Buffy, but fortunately, lying is not one of them."

Relief washed over Buffy and she felt suddenly weak, as though she might fall down. She swallowed hard and sat down. "Oh. Oh, God. I thought—"

"I'm sorry," Giles said kindly. "I needed her to think that I was on her side. I don't know how far she'll take this charade."

Buffy raised her eyebrows. "Try far," she rasped, still filled with emotion. "Like all the way."

Giles moved to sit across from her. "You should have come to me right off," he chastised her.

"I know," she said softly. "I wanted to."

"But Faith wouldn't hear of it."

"It's not all her fault, Giles," Buffy explained grimly. "We both thought it was a vampire. I only realized a second before—"

"Buffy, this is not the first time something like this has happened."

She blinked. "It isn't?"

He leaned in, trying to comfort her. "A Slayer is on the front line of a nightly war. It's tragic, but accidents have happened."

"What do you do?"

"Well, the Council investigates, metes out punishment if punishment is due. But I have no plan to involve them," he revealed. "It's the last thing Faith needs at the moment. She's unstable, Buffy. She's utterly unable to accept responsibility."

Buffy stared at the carpet. "She's freaking. So . . . then we just have to help her deal, right?"

"She's in denial. There *is* no help for her until she admits what happened."

"I could talk to her," Buffy suggested.

Giles mulled that over. "Perhaps."

"Or maybe," Buffy went on, "maybe I'm too close. Maybe one of the guys could?"

"We should meet," Giles decided. "I mean, it may be that they're seeing a different side of her."

"Okay."

"In the meantime, no one else is to know, understood?"

"Okay."

Just a few feet inside the library door, Wesley stood listening, a cold, grim certainty filling him. He had seen Faith leaving, and had come in only a moment later. The young Watcher had overheard everything, not the least of which was their intention to keep it all from him.

"This is extremely delicate," Giles continued. "If we scare her off now, we may lose her forever."

CHAPTER 3

In the modest hotel room where he had been staying since his arrival in Sunnydale, Wesley hesitated only a moment before picking up the phone. He dialed quickly, then waited the extra few seconds it always took for an international call to be put through. Finally, on the other end, an ominous male voice answered.

"Hello?"

"Yes, hello," Wesley said quickly. "Mr. Travers, please. Quentin Travers. Wesley Wyndam-Pryce calling."

"What's the code word?"

"The code word?" Wesley replied, momentarily taken aback. Then he remembered. "Monkey."

"Spell it."

"M-O-N-K . . . just put him on, will you? This is an emergency."

The next afternoon, when school had let out, Buffy, Giles, Willow and Xander gathered in the cafeteria to discuss their next move. The place was empty, the floor long since mopped, the chairs put up on tables. They spread out and regarded each other silently, each contemplating the situation with Faith, and no one coming up with a happy ending.

"Maybe we should all talk to Faith together," Willow suggested.

"You mean like that intervention thing you guys did on me?" Buffy replied. "As I recall, Xander and I nearly came to blows."

Xander glanced up. He was sitting on a chair that was still on top of a table, and yet somehow did not look absurd. "You nearly came to blows, Buffy," he reminded her. "I nearly came to loss of limbs."

"No, Faith is too defensive for a confrontation like that," Giles observed. "She'd respond better to a one-on-one approach."

"I could be the one," Xander offered. "On her one. Um, let's rephrase. I think she might listen to me. We kind of have a . . . connection."

Buffy shot him a dubious look. "A connection? Why would you think that?"

"I'm just saying it's worth a shot. That's all."

Giles frowned. "I don't see it, Xander. I mean, of all of us, you're the one person, arguably, that Faith has had the least contact with."

"Yeah, but we hung out a little. Recently. And she seemed to be, uh, responsive," Xander explained.

"When did you guys hang out?" Buffy asked.

Xander fidgeted a bit. "She was fighting one of those apocalypse demon things and I helped her. Gave her a ride home."

"And you guys talked?"

"Not extensively."

Buffy shook her head. "Then why would you . . . oh."
Giles's eyebrows shot up. "Oh!"

They all looked to Willow for her response. Buffy's heart went out to her friend. Willow loved Oz now, he was her boyfriend. And she knew Willow would never change that for anything. But she also knew that Willow had loved Xander for years, had been his best friend almost his entire life, and had once dreamed that when it finally happened, it would be the two of them.

Willow tried to put on a brave face, but her sadness was plain to Buffy.

"I don't need to say 'oh,'" she said calmly. "I got it before. They slept together."

Giles stared at her for a moment, then shifted uncomfortably in his chair. "Fine, then. Let's move on."

"Look, I know that you mean well, Xander," Buffy began, "but I just don't see Faith opening up to you. She doesn't take the guys she . . . has a connection with . . . very seriously. They're kind of a big joke to her. No offense."

Xander snorted derisively. "Oh, no. Why would I be offended by that?"

"However, if you still want to be of assistance," Giles put in, "I need some help with research. There's still the business of the Mayor and Mr. Trick to attend to."

"Yeah," Buffy agreed. "They seemed pretty cozy the other night."

"Willow?" Giles asked. "Can you access the Mayor's files?"

"What?" Willow replied, in a bit of a daze. "Oh, sure. I can try."

Giles rose from his chair. "Good. Clearly we need to take a harder look at him. He's obviously up to something."

He tipped the chair upside down and put it back on top of the table behind him.

"What about Faith?" Buffy prodded.

That stopped him. "I don't know," Giles confessed. "I need time."

"She needs help now," Buffy said quickly. "I owe her that."

When they'd all gone off to wherever they needed to be next, Willow went into the women's bathroom. She took a stall right in the middle, put the lid of the toilet down, and sat. It was only a moment before the tears came.

The sound of her crying echoed off the tile walls and she tried to stifle it as much as possible.

It was silly. She knew that. But the knowledge did not stop the clutching pain in her heart, or drive away the alarming feeling that she could not catch her breath.

She loved Oz. He loved her. But everything the little girl part of Willow had ever innocently believed about the sweetness of love was tied up in her feelings for Xander, in a way she would never have been able to put into words. It was special to her, this thing that Xander had thrown away on a cold, heartless girl who cared nothing for him.

So it was not the high school senior, college-bound Willow who sat in that bathroom stall, heartbroken, lost in her disappointment. It was the little girl who'd day-dreamed romance since the second grade.

That little girl wept long and lonely.

Xander wanted to help. He was stung by what Buffy had said, guilt-ridden from the expression on Willow's face when she'd learned the truth, and more than a little concerned for Faith. He had known she was a wild one, but murder? He could not even imagine it.

Still, he paused for a moment in front of the door to her motel room, wondering if he was doing the right thing. The others had warned him off. But, then again, they did have a tendency to underestimate him. And only he could know what it had been like, him and Faith together. They *did* have a connection.

Car horns beeped out on the main road and headlights cut the night. Xander knocked. He could hear the TV on inside. Before he could knock again, the door swung open.

Faith was breathtaking. She always looked hot, but she stood there with her hair pinned up, dark eyeliner punctuating her sultry gaze, in a shirt that revealed her taut stomach, and a pair of black leather pants that had a devastating effect.

"What?" she barked.

Xander blinked, took a breath. "I just . . . came by to see how you are, actually."

"Sick of people asking me that, for one thing."

He rubbed a hand across his face, uncertain how to proceed. "Can I come in? Just to talk, I promise."

Faith smirked. "Like you could make something happen if I didn't want it to?"

"Hey, yeah," he replied with a nervous laugh. "Got me there. Pretty much not gonna try to 'take you' under any circumstances." He made a muscle. "See? Here, feel that. Probably like a wet noodle to you."

Reluctantly, she stepped aside to let him in. "Five minutes."

"That's all I need," Xander promised as he entered. "For talking. In conversation, I'm quick as a bunny."

Faith shut the door behind him. "Clock is running."

"Yeah. It's just, I heard about what happened and I thought you might need a friend."

"So then go talk to Buffy," she replied, arms crossed in front of her. "She's the one who killed a guy."

Xander hesitated for a moment. "Yeah. I heard that version."

"Version?" Faith snapped.

"Either way, it sounds like it was an accident, and that's the important part."

Faith cocked her head to one side, all attitude. "No.

The important part is that *Buffy* is the *accidental* murderer."

After a moment of stumbling around for the words, Xander decided just to forge ahead. "Faith, you may not think so, but I sort of know you. I've seen you post-battle. And I know firsthand that you're like a wild thing and half the time you don't know what you're doing."

"And you're living proof of that, aren't you?" The smile on Faith's lips was not a pleasant one.

"See, you can try to hurt me, but right now you need someone on your side," he insisted. "It wasn't your fault. I'm willing to testify to that, in court, if you need me."

"You'd like that, wouldn't you? To get up in front of all your geek pals and go on record about how I made you my boy toy for a night."

Xander frowned. "No. No, that's not it."

"I know what this is all about," Faith replied. She moved in a little closer, reached up to run her fingers across his chest. "You just came by here 'cause you want another taste."

She moved in to kiss him, and for a moment, Xander almost complied. But then he shook his head and pulled back.

"No. It was nice. It was great. It . . . was kind of a blur. But, okay, someday, sure, yay. But not now. Not like this."

She gazed at him seductively, slipped her hands behind his neck and began to move against him. "Like how, then? Lights on or off? Kinks or vanilla?"

Xander backed away. "Faith, come on! I came here to help you." He gazed at her sadly. "I thought we had a connection."

She giggled like a little girl. Then she grabbed him by the front of his shirt and threw him violently down onto the bed. Faith straddled him, trapping him beneath her.

"You want to feel our connection? It's just skin," she said as she pulled his shirt up. "I see. I want. I take." She kissed him, deeply, passionately, moving against him on the bed. Then Faith looked into his eyes. "I forget."

"No . . . we . . . it was more than that."

"I could do anything to you right now, and you want me to." Faith kissed him again, bit down on his lower lip. Her hands slipped around his throat and she began to squeeze. "I could make you die."

Xander gasped, tried to speak, but Faith was choking him. He thought, for an instant, it was a sick joke. Then he saw the look in her eyes and he panicked. She wasn't just choking him. She was killing him. Xander tried to fight her, reached up to push her away, but she was a Slayer. Her strength was so much greater than his. Blackness began to creep into the edges of his vision. Fireworks went off in his brain.

Xander gazed up at her in terror.

The motel room door opened and closed. Xander glanced beyond Faith to see a dark figure standing behind her.

Angel.

Faith turned toward him, and Angel cracked her across the face with a baseball bat.

Before Faith even opened her eyes, she felt the cold iron around her wrists. She shifted slightly, and heard the chains clank together. When she opened her eyes, she saw Angel sitting nearby on a bench, toying with the baseball bat he'd used to knock her out.

The ball of ice that had been growing ever larger inside her since she had killed Allan Finch shot spikes of cold all through her. She expected Buffy and Giles to react the way they had. They just did not understand. It had been hard for her to deal with at first, but she was over it.

The rules the rest of the world followed did not apply to Slayers. Buffy couldn't see it; that made her weak.

Finch's death was regrettable, but Faith would not allow herself to lose sleep over it, would not allow herself to care. That would be like admitting she had done something *wrong*.

And that would make *her* weak. She could not afford to ever be weak again.

So she expected it from Buffy and Giles. But from Angel? He knew what it was like to live beyond the rules set up by normal humans, by weak-willed losers who did not know what it was like to have the kind of power she had. Angel should have been on her side. He should have been with her in all the ways that mattered.

Buffy, with her judgments and her code of honor, was just not the woman for him.

"Finally decided to tie me up, huh?" Faith taunted the vampire flirtatiously. "Always knew you weren't really a one-Slayer guy."

"Sorry about the chains," Angel said, voice low. "It's not that I don't trust you . . . actually, it *is* that I don't trust you."

Angel set the bat aside. *The bat.* Faith realized that Angel was upset about what he had walked in on. But she figured after the knock on the head he had given her, they were even.

"The thing with Xander?" Faith offered. "I know what it looked like, but we were just playing."

"And he forgot the safety word? Is that it?" Angel rose and strode toward her.

"Safety words are for wusses," Faith muttered.

All of a sudden her interest in Angel dissipated. Whatever he might once have been, all the time he had spent with Buffy had weakened him. It was obvious that he, too, expected Faith to live by the so-called rules. Faith was on her own, always on her own. But, then, that was the simplest way to be. The safest way.

Angel crouched in front of her, eyes hard. "I bet you're not big on trust games, are you, Faith?"

Faith scoffed. "You gonna shrink me now, that it?"

"No. I just want to talk to you."

Chains clinking, she moved toward him a bit, as much as her bonds would allow. Maybe Angel thought he was a white hat these days, but Faith had learned the hard way that nobody was really that good. Everyone had an agenda; everyone worked an angle. With men, all the angles usually came down to one thing.

"That's what they all say," she told him. "And then it's 'just let me stay the night. I won't try anything.' "

"You want to go the long way around? Hey, I can do that," Angel said nonchalantly. He stood up and turned to walk away. "I'm not getting any older."

As Angel walked away, Faith stared at his back. She felt despair creeping into her mind and body again, but she froze it out, forced it away. *Saving the world's gotta count for something,* she told herself. *The rules have to bend.*

Angel left the room, and Faith dropped her gaze. *How do you do it, Angel?* she thought in wonder. *How do you just walk around like none of the horrible things you did ever happened?*

Buffy sat on a stone bench in the garden patio. She could hear muffled talking inside, so she knew that Faith was awake. A minute or so after that, Angel's heavy footfalls echoed out to her, and she glanced up to see him emerge from the house. She stood to greet him.

"How's she doing?"

His expression was grim, even more brooding than usual. "Like talking to a wall. Only you get more from a wall."

"But you'll keep trying, right?" Buffy asked hopefully.

"Sure. We're just getting started."

"So what do I do?" she asked.

Angel shook his head. It was obvious he thought she didn't get it. The thing was, Buffy knew enough about herself to realize that she simply did not want to get it.

"Look, right now there's nothing you can do," Angel told her.

"Well, this could take a while right? So I'll just go to Faith's and I'll get some of her stuff. That way she'll see that we're on her side."

"That's a good idea," Angel allowed.

"Great. I'll be right back." She started to turn, but Angel stopped her.

"Look, I . . . I don't want you to get your hopes up, Buffy. She may not want us to help her."

"She does," Buffy insisted. "She just doesn't know how to say it."

"She killed a man," Angel said gravely. "That changes everything for her."

Buffy shook her head. "Giles said with counseling, they might not even need to lock her up."

"That's not what I mean," Angel replied, eyes soft and gentle.

Looking at him, then, Buffy realized that she had been wrong. Maybe he was right. Maybe she really didn't get it at all.

"She's taken a life," Angel reminded her. He glanced down.

"I know."

He lifted his gaze to her again, dark knowledge in his eyes. "She's got a taste for it now."

The Mayor stood in the middle of his office, hands stuffed into his pants pockets, furious as he watched a security camera tape of the corridor just outside his office. Behind him, Trick waited silently.

"Not one Slayer, but two," the Mayor observed, as he

watched Buffy and Faith sneak into the late Deputy Mayor's office. "Right here in the building."

"There was supposed to be a guard," Trick said defensively.

"Ssshh," the Mayor replied. "Here comes my favorite part, where the Slayers see us in the hall together, thick as thieves. Oh, wait, we are thieves! And worse. And now they know it," he snapped.

"They're not gonna be much of a threat in jail."

"We don't have near enough evidence to put them away," the Mayor explained, eyes still locked on the video screen. "No, you're going to have to come up with a more efficient solution. And, Mr. Trick, you'd better think of it soon."

The Mayor did not even turn to regard the vampire, but he was quite certain that Trick had gotten the message.

Angel stared down at Faith and shuddered. He saw a bit of himself in her. The part of himself he spent every single day trying to make up for.

"I know what's going on with you," he told her.

"Join the club," she replied dully. "Everybody seems to have a theory."

Revulsion rose in him, for his own actions, and for Faith's. And yet just as he believed he could find his own redemption, he hoped it was not too late for Faith to turn back and try to find hers.

"But I know," he said. "What it's like to take a life. To feel a future, a world of possibility, snuffed out by your own hand. I know the power in it. The exhilaration. It was like a drug for me."

"Yeah?" Faith asked with mock sincerity. "Sounds like you need some help. A professional, maybe."

Angel strode to the bench in front of the blazing fire and sat down. "A professional couldn't have helped me. It stopped when I got my soul back. My human heart."

"Goody for you," she sneered. Then, as if searching for sympathy, she moved forward, holding her shackled hands up to him. "If we're going to party, let's get on with it. Otherwise, could you let me out of these things?"

"Faith, you have a choice. You've tasted something few ever do. To kill without remorse is to feel like a god—"

She thrashed against the chains. "Right now, all I feel is a cramp in my wrist. Let me go!"

Angel walked to her again and crouched down. His nostrils flared as he studied her. "But you're not a god," he went on, ignoring her protests. "No. You're not much more than a child. And going down this path will ruin you. You can't imagine the price for true evil."

For just a moment, a flicker, he thought his words might have sunk in. But then her eyes glazed over again.

"Yeah? I hope evil takes Mastercard."

"You and me, Faith, we're a lot alike," Angel told her. He rose and began to pace a bit. "Time was, I thought humans existed just to hurt each other."

All the dark humor drained from Faith's expression. Her face was pale, dead. She would not meet his gaze. Angel sat beside her and leaned against the wall.

"But then I came here. And I found out that there are other types of people. People who genuinely wanted to do right."

Angel glanced at her, opening up. Faith did not look away this time, her eyes large and lost.

"They make mistakes," Angel allowed. "They fall down. But they keep caring. Keep trying. If you can trust us, Faith, this could all change. You don't have to disappear into the darkness."

Angel was sure he had reached her, that he had at least begun to chip away at the hurt that she had cocooned herself in. Faith was in a dark place, but he knew in that moment that she could still be saved.

The doors burst open and Wesley rushed in with a trio of thugs in his wake. Angel ran at them, but Wesley lifted a cross to ward him off. Angel backpedaled for only a second, but it was enough. One of the thugs decked him with a hard right and a second threw a net over him. He thrashed against the netting, but he only became more tangled. The third began to beat him with a crowbar and Angel grunted with each blow.

Through the mesh across his face, he watched as Wesley took the shackles off Faith, then handcuffed her with his own chains. Faith stared at him in astonishment.

"What?" she asked, stunned.

"By the order of the Watchers Council of Britain," Wesley announced, "I am exercising my authority and removing you to England, where you will accept the judgment of the disciplinary committee."

Wesley and the thugs dragged her out, and Faith barely fought them. Angel writhed in pain, wrapped in the net, but his thoughts were not of himself. They were of Faith. He had gotten through; he knew he had.

But after this new betrayal, he feared she was truly lost to them forever.

CHAPTER 4

It was a boxy delivery truck, with plenty of room in back. But the only cargo it carried were Faith, Wesley, and one of the Council thugs he'd brought with him. She sat across from the two men, but she barely registered their presence. Faith stared at nothing, numb to everything. The engine rumbled and the truck rolled along, and she turned off the entire world, descended down into herself.

In her whole life she had never known anybody she could trust. Then, when she was chosen to receive the powers and abilities of the Slayer, that had seemed to change. Her first Watcher had trained her well. They had begun to grow close, and the woman had vowed to stick by Faith. But then they had gone up against Kakistos and her Watcher had been killed. It was not as though she thought the woman had chosen death; she was not stupid. But Faith had still felt as though she had been abandoned. Betrayed. Lied to.

She had been alone again.

The Council of Watchers was not done with her yet,

however. Faith had allowed herself to trust Buffy, and Giles, and Mrs. Post, and even Angel, a little bit.

One by one, they had all abandoned her.

Now the Council of Watchers, having taunted her with the perverse fantasy that such things as truth and honesty and loyalty might actually exist . . . now they wanted to punish *her* for one little mistake.

Faith would have laughed if she wasn't so sure it would make her throw up.

"I'm sorry for the extreme measures," Wesley said, his usual pompous self. "Unfortunately, this is a rather extreme circumstance."

"Whatever," she drawled.

"Please believe, nobody is rushing to judgment," he went on. "The first priority of both myself and the Council is to help you."

Faith had run her hands along the chains that restrained her, and found that they were bolted to iron rings that jutted from the bench. She gripped the rings and twisted, trying to pull them loose.

"Ah, now, none of that," Wesley warned her. He turned to the Council operative seated beside him. "Tighten her restraints."

The operative rose and reached toward Faith.

Wesley continued. "Faith, there's no point in fighting this, you know—"

Faith nailed the operative between the legs with a solid kick. The man cried out in agony and went down hard. He'd barely bounced off the floor when she slammed a boot down on the side of his head and looked up at Wesley with a snarl.

"Have to disagree with you on that one. Now unlock these or I'll pop this guy's head like a grape."

Wesley's eyes ticked to a wrench that lay on the floor of the truck. Faith caught the look.

"Don't even think about it," she warned.

With no further hesitation, but with a sickened look on his face, Wesley rose and searched his pockets for the key. He found it, and unlocked her cuffs.

"Faith, you can't keep running," he told her.

She hit him so hard she was surprised—and a little disappointed—that she didn't feel his jaw give way. Wesley went down on his belly, right by the wrench. His fingers wrapped around it, and he turned, about to attack.

Faith grabbed his wrist midswing, pulled him toward her, and head-butted him. Their skulls cracked together, and Wesley fell unconscious to the floor of the truck.

"Wrong again, Wes," she said tiredly.

Then she turned, kicked the rear doors of the truck open, and leaped out without even waiting for it to slow. She hit the pavement, rolled, and then was up and running.

Fleeing into the darkness.

In the school library, Angel paced angrily. Buffy had freed him and they had gone immediately to find Giles. He and Willow and Xander had been doing research on Mr. Trick and the Mayor, but Buffy and Angel's news took immediate precedence.

"It was the new Watcher," Angel confirmed. "He had a couple of guys with him."

"Then he figured it out," Willow observed.

"Which means that Faith will be soon on her way to England to face the Watchers Council," Giles informed them.

Though they were inside now, Buffy still felt cold. "And then what?"

"Most likely, they'll lock her away for a good long while," Giles replied.

"So we head 'em off at the airport and stop them," Buffy announced.

Willow shook her head. "Can I . . . I'm just wondering. Why? I'm not the most objective, I know. I kinda have an issue with Faith sharing my people. But she murdered someone and accused Buffy. Then she hurt Xander. I hate to say it, but maybe she belongs behind bars."

Buffy nodded slowly. "She's out of control, I know. But Angel was getting somewhere with her. She was opening up. If we could just stop Wesley—"

Her words ended abruptly. Buffy stared at the doors to the library. Wesley stood just inside.

"That's no longer an issue," he admitted.

"You let her get away?" Buffy asked, eyes wide.

" 'Let' wouldn't be the way I'd phrase it, but yes, she escaped."

"Good work," Angel snapped. "First you terrorize her, then you put her back on the streets."

"That was hardly my plan," Wesley argued. "I was trying to save the girl—"

Buffy railed at him. "But you didn't! You probably destroyed her."

Softly, Giles said her name. "Buffy, that's enough," he told her.

The Slayer took a long breath, then let it out. "We'd better find her before she does any more damage." She rose, glanced around the room, and began to issue orders. "We should split up. I'll check the docks; that's probably where she is. Giles, why don't you go to her motel. Xander, Willow, her haunts. And be *careful.*"

She turned to Angel, but he was already in motion. "I'll try the airport."

"What can I do?" Wesley asked. "I want to help."

Buffy glared at him for a moment, then brushed past him, headed for the door. "Still got your ticket back to the mother country?"

* * *

Freighters and fishing boats were crowded up against the ocean docks like a city unto themselves. Faith waited on the deck of an enormous freighter, heavily laden with its cargo. It would depart soon, and then she could put all of it, all of *them*, behind her.

She paced the deck for a time, and her gaze kept drifting back to the docks, until she was forced to ask herself what she was looking for. The answer was simple; she knew Buffy did not give up easily. So Faith was not surprised when she saw the other Slayer walking along the dock, glancing around at the shadows, obviously searching—or hunting—for her.

"You don't give up, do you?" Faith asked, stepping from the shadows of the deck.

"Not on my friends, no," Buffy said, painfully earnest.

"Yeah, 'cause you and me are such solid buds."

"We could be," Buffy offered. "It's not too late."

"For me to change, and be more like you, you mean?" Faith scoffed. "Little Miss Goody Two Shoes? It ain't gonna happen, B."

"Faith, no one's asking you to be more like me, but you can't go on like this."

Faith grinned. "Scares you, doesn't it?" She climbed down the gangway to the dock and walked toward Buffy.

"Yeah, it scares me. Faith, you're hurting people. You're hurting yourself."

"But that's not it," Faith said quickly, growing angry and yet also certain she understood the situation much better than Buffy did. "That's not what bothers you so much. What bugs you is, you know I'm right. You know in your gut, we don't need the law. We *are* the law."

Buffy turned and strode away. "No."

Faith considered it a little victory, forcing Buffy to see the truth of it. Thrilled, she pursued the other Slayer.

"Yes. You know exactly what I'm about because you have it in you, too."

"No, Faith, you're sick," Buffy said, her voice cold and sad. She picked up her pace, unwilling to listen.

Faith liked that. If Buffy found her words frightening, Faith figured maybe she was getting through. "I've seen it, B. You've got the lust. And I'm not just talking about screwing vampires."

Buffy whirled on her, enraged. "Don't you dare bring him into this."

A rush of excitement went through Faith, and she licked her lips. "It was good, wasn't it? The sex? The danger? Bet a part of you even dug him when he went psycho."

"No," Buffy said again. She walked away.

Once more, Faith pursued her. "See, you need me to tow the line because you're afraid you'll go over it, aren't you, B? You can't handle watching me living my own way, having a blast, because it *tempts* you. You know it could *be* you."

Something snapped inside Buffy. The other Slayer spun, cocked back her fist, and hit Faith so hard she spun around. When she faced Buffy again, Faith touched her split lip, smiling.

"There's my girl," she said happily. It was exactly what she had wanted, to force Buffy to let the bad girl out, to see that they truly were two of a kind.

"No," Buffy said suddenly, and picked up her pace, walking away again. "I'm not going to do this," she vowed.

"Why not?" Faith taunted her. "It feels good. Blood rising . . ."

She let her words trail off and her smile widened as she cut off Buffy's path. Suddenly, from above, she heard the clanking of metal. Faith looked up to see a crane swing an enormous wooden crate out above them.

The crate was released. It crashed down toward them.

Buffy shoved Faith out of the way and then dove, but the crate slammed down on her back, trapping her beneath it. Faith actually got up and moved to help her.

Then the vampires swarmed in. Mr. Trick was there, but there were three others as well. With Buffy trapped, they rushed at Faith. Trick and another grabbed her and tossed her backward. Then they surrounded her. The four vampires attacked as though they expected her to be easy pickings, but Faith was hardly that.

Buffy blinked, her mind a fog as she watched the fight. Dazed, she tried to free herself, but whatever was in the crate was heavy.

Every blow she took, Faith dished out two. The crack of her fist on flesh echoed through the night and out across the ocean. One of the vampires grabbed her from behind and another ran at her. Faith dropped down out of her captor's grasp, and the two slammed into one another. She fended off two more attacks, then grabbed one of the vampires and threw him off the dock. He screamed as he plummeted down into the ocean.

She kept fighting. But Buffy knew that it was doubtful she could win alone. By sheer force of will, she inched the crate up off her legs and slid out. Weakened, she dragged herself to her feet, and glanced up.

Mr. Trick slammed a fist into her face, and Buffy was knocked back into a stack of smaller crates. They tumbled down around her.

Woozy, she climbed to her feet. She took a couple of swings at Trick, but he got in another hard shot. Buffy was not prepared for this fight. She needed a couple of minutes to recover, to shake it off. But Trick was not going to give her that.

Buffy only hoped that by drawing Trick away, she had given Faith the opening she needed with the other two.

Growling like a beast, Trick wrapped a length of cord around Buffy's neck and began to choke her. He dragged her across the ground, then swung her up against another stack of crates.

Faith would either die, or she would win, and then leave. Buffy tried to summon her strength, knowing she would have to save herself. But there was no strength there to summon. Trick snarled as he grabbed her by the throat.

"I hear once you've tasted a Slayer, you never wanna go back," he told her.

Eyes blazing yellow, fangs gleaming by moonlight, he dropped his mouth to her throat, and Buffy felt his teeth graze her flesh.

There came a shout from behind him, and then a familiar, wet, crunching sound. Trick stiffened and looked up at Buffy in disbelief.

"Oh, no. No, this is no good at all," he moaned. Then he exploded in a tiny cloud of ash.

Faith stood behind him, stake in hand.

Epilogue

So she saved you?"

Giles poured Buffy a cup of tea. It was very late, and the library seemed haunted by the ghosts of all they had been through in the long weeks since Faith had first arrived in Sunnydale.

"She could have left me there to die, Giles. But she didn't."

He nodded once. "She opted to come back to town with you. That bodes well. She still has a lot to face before she can put this behind her."

"I'm not gonna give up on her," Buffy said firmly.

Giles poured his own tea, then regarded her warmly. "Then I think she stands a chance."

Buffy smiled, just a bit.

The Mayor slipped on his coat. It had been a very late night, but then he had a lot of work to do. Running a city like Sunnydale while planning a demonic Ascension, well, it was a lot for any one man to handle.

He opened his office door and found Faith standing in the corridor, glaring at him.

"You sent your boy to kill me," she sneered.

"That's right. I did."

"He's dust."

"I thought he might be," the Mayor said easily. "What with you standing here and all."

Faith took two steps forward, invading his personal space. "I guess that means you have a job opening."

With an ironic smile, the Mayor stepped aside to let Faith enter.

Then he closed the door.

ABOUT THE AUTHOR

James Laurence is an attorney and freelance writer who lives in Baltimore, Maryland. This is his first *Buffy* novelization.

They're real, and they're here...

When Jack Dwyer's best friend Artie is murdered, he is devastated. But his world is turned upside down when Artie emerges from the ghostlands to bring him a warning.

With his dead friend's guidance, Jack learns of the Prowlers. They move from city to city, preying on humans until they are close to being exposed, then they move on.

Jack wants revenge. But even as he hunts the Prowlers, he marks himself— and all of his loved ones—as prey.

Don't miss the exciting new series from

BESTSELLING AUTHOR CHRISTOPHER GOLDEN!

PROWLERS